Circle of Friends

The Camelot Rabbitry Series
Volume Three

By
Jeanette Adams

Circle of Friends

The Camelot Rabbitry Series
Volume Three

by Jeanette Adams

Printed by:
Network Printers
Milwaukee, WI

Edited by Bert Adams & Lisa D'Angelo
Copyright 2006 by Jeanette Adams
Cover art copyright 2006 by Jeanette Adams

Website: www.talesfromwithin.com

Library of Congress Control Number: 2006908605

ISBN 10: 0-9672375-3-X (pbk.)
ISBN 13: 978-0-9672375-3-4 (pbk.)

Contents

The Chrysanthemum Leaves

Chapter 1

It was early morning and Bilbo, Cody, Juliet and Double Delight were awakened by the sound of unfamiliar music. As they rubbed the sleep from their eyes, they could see Natsumi crouched on the floor next to a small phonograph. She was writing on the flower petals she had gathered the day before. The rabbits watched, enchanted by the twanging of an old Japanese instrumental.

Bilbo could feel Sensei, the silkworm, stirring on the back of his neck. "Hello there! Are you awake, Sensei?" Bilbo called out.

"Yes, but I'm so hungry," Sensei grumbled, as he smacked his small grub-like lips in search of food.

"What is Natsumi doing?" Bilbo asked curiously.

"She must be writing Kannon Sutra verses on the chrysanthemum leaves," Sensei replied. "It is said that if one writes four verses on a chrysanthemum leaf, the dew will form an elixir that will bring one thousand years of life."

"That's not really possible, is it?" Bilbo questioned.

"Oh, but it's quite true! I have drunk the elixir and have lived many centuries in spite of the fact that a silk worm's life consists of a matter of days. Many things have yet to be understood in this world, Bilbo. How do you think it is possible that we are able to understand one another's language? There are unexplained things at work here."

"But Sensei, why would Natsumi worry about such things?" Double D asked.

"Her grandfather just recently passed away. I think she wishes she could've prevented it and hopes she may save other loved ones from the same fate."

1

Natsumi finished her writing. As she tucked her dark hair behind her ears, they watched her small fingers wrap the leaves inside a piece of tissue paper. She then placed the tissue safely behind the stone-lined pool of water inside the small bonsai garden that sat next to the rabbit's cage.

"There, now I will have done like Kikujido, no more will there be sickness," Natsumi said out loud.

"I'll never forget the first time Grandfather Riujin spoke to me," Sensei whispered. "One day in Kamakura, while Natsumi was taking her afternoon nap, he slipped into her room and whispered, 'Little dragon, I have brought you something to eat.' At first, I didn't answer, but after several more days of him slipping eucalyptus leaves into her backpack for me, I finally spoke out. 'Dear Grandfather Riujin, how is it you know of my humble existence?' I asked. He replied, 'Since before my time the story has been told of a young girl, a little dragon, and a rabbit, which together save the world from demons. You are that dragon and it is I who must train you for your destiny,' he explained. I'll never understand why he liked to call me little dragon, but from that day on, I learned there is much that goes on in this world that can't be explained."

"Everything is happening so fast, Sensei," Bilbo whispered back. "You think that I'm supposed to help save the world from demons? What happens if I can't?"

"It could mean the end of the world we know. Evil would rule the world and all that you know of would be gone. But right now I think we should focus on the present and what can be done."

They were suddenly interrupted by Natsumi's chatter. "Now Bilbo, what do you think I have here?" Natsumi asked, as she peered into the cage at him.

Bilbo looked up in surprise. "How could she know that I'm Bilbo and not Binky? No one ever noticed that I switched places with him," he thought to himself.

"Yes, I know you're really not Binky! Look here, I got a letter from your keeper that tells me all! How clever you were to come to Japan with Double Delight! Now you can always be with me! Your keeper says that it's okay, that you can stay with me forever now," Natsumi said, as she opened the rabbit's cage door.

"Come here, let me hold you close," she beckoned. Bilbo hopped across the cage and into Natsumi's waiting arms. Natsumi cradled him and drew him close to her face.

"Bilbo, I told my grandfather all about you and he says you were sent to me. He says it's destiny that you've come to Japan and you are to become a great hero," Natsumi cooed, closing her little eyes, as she caressed his soft fur.

"What do you think I have planned for today?" she asked a very bewildered Bilbo. "It's okay, you can talk. I know you can talk to me like Snowflake," Natsumi instructed.

Bilbo looked first at Natsumi and then at Double D.

"I think it's okay, Bilbo," Sensei's voice called out from beneath Bilbo's hair. "I'm sure we can talk to Natsumi as long as she doesn't tell anyone else about it."

"Bilbo, whose voice is that?" asked a puzzled Natsumi.

"That is Sensei, our silkworm friend," Bilbo answered.

"Bilbo, it's true, you can talk!" exclaimed an ecstatic Natsumi. "And you have a silkworm friend that also talks?"

"Yes, Natsumi. It is time you know. I used to come with you to Kamakura, and your grandfather used to talk with me," Sensei explained.

"But why didn't you speak to me before?" Natsumi asked.

"Your grandfather instructed me to speak only when the right time came."

"So you can understand different languages, too, like Grandfather taught me?" asked a puzzled Natsumi. "I didn't know silkworms could talk. Also, I can't understand how you have lived so long."

"The chrysanthemum leaves. I knew of the story long before you were born because your grandfather used them on me. He and I talked for long periods of time while you were taking your naps. He told me many stories of the past and of the future to come," Sensei explained.

"Well, this is going to be so much fun!" Natsumi exclaimed. "Today is Sunday. We'll all go to Ueno Park and have a great time! We'll have to bring my brother, Toshi, though."

"Can we talk to Toshi without him telling anyone?" Sensei asked nervously.

"I'm not sure, but my mom won't let me go without him and we need him to help pull the carrier. All my friends will be waiting to see my new rabbits."

"Well, why don't we get going?" Bilbo asked.

"All right. I'll go find Toshi and then we'll be off," Natsumi agreed, as she set Bilbo and the others down inside their travel carrier.

"You can all come to see the park. I'll go get the travel dolly," Natsumi said, as she left the room.

A few minutes later, a juvenile boy with choppy dark bangs entered the room.

"Why do I always have to do stuff for you? I have a life too," he grumbled as he hastily gathered the carrier to bring downstairs.

A Stroll Through Ueno Park

Chapter 2

Soon, they were outside the front door in the sunshine. Natsumi covered the top of the carrier with an imitation Bamboo shrine that she and Toshi used to play with. This concealed the rabbits very well. She then placed a toy-sized taiko drum on top to complete the disguise. Toshi pulled the dolly along the sidewalk, heading toward the path that led across the pond area of Ueno Park. In Japan, this was the first pond they had seen, but today it looked cheery and carefree. They passed the boathouse and the rabbits watched as their cart rolled by Benton-do Shrine, outside of which the traditional pot of incense was burning.

"This is the way I always take to go to Ueno Park," Natsumi explained, as they began to walk down a land bridge that led from the Benton-do Temple area. Rows of large iron lanterns lined the walkway on their journey. "I think it's one of the prettiest parts of the park."

They crossed Zoo-dori Avenue and stood on the opposite side of the street, under the tree-lined roadway.

"Which way now?" Toshi complained. "There are stairs whichever way we go."

"Why don't we go by way of Kannon-do Temple? There are lots of little shrines there that the rabbits could hop right into without being spotted. I would like to take them to my favorite Shinto shrine," Natsumi instructed, as they approached the street outside.

Toshi and Natsumi crossed the street and then together, lifted the little wagon in order to take the direct path through the Tori Gate and up the hill. Reaching the hilltop, they sat for a moment watching tourists as they caught their breath. A monk passed by them on his way to the temple.

"Where is it you want to go?" Toshi asked.

5

"Follow me. Grandfather always liked the small Shinto shrine that is built on top of a ceramic mountain. He used to take me there often. It's not crowded and it's much quieter there."

It was quite beautiful in the forest as Bilbo and the others peered out of their carrier at the clean, well-marked paths. "Somehow, I don't think there are coyotes here," Cody commented.

"You'd better not think you're going to escape in the park, you bunnies. Grandfather told me that there are demon tanuki that lurk here in the night!" Natsumi warned.

"There is no such thing, you dummy!" Toshi exclaimed.

"Think what you may, but Grandfather knew a lot of things about the ancient ways that no one else did."

"Ancient ways being the clue word there! Most of those stories are a bunch of wives tales!" Toshi complained.

"Well, maybe someday you won't be so quick to dismiss them when they start coming true…"

"Here we are!" Natsumi announced, as she rolled the cart to a stop inside a small building. To the right, the rabbits could see many fox-like ceramic figurines decorating a ledge where incense was burned. In the center of the room, there was a small wooden shrine, similar to the large temples outside. It was built upon a rock formation that resembled a mountaintop. They watched as Natsumi lit some incense and then approached the small shrine. As she did, she clapped her hands to wake the gods. They watched Natsumi as she stood quietly and then bowed. From the look on her face, they could only think that she was praying for her grandfather.

"We'll come back here tonight if you don't mind," Sensei whispered into Bilbo's ear. "This looks like where Grandfather Riujin described when he told me to take my newfound rabbit friend here…for some reason that I don't know. Maybe when we come here we'll figure out what the meaning of all this is."

Natsumi soon turned around and was ready to go. Their cart made its way out of the shrine and into the park, rolling past a Buddhist pagoda and the statue of Prince Komatsu.

From within the cart, the rabbits could see a giant fountain as the children turned toward the main gate of the zoo entrance. Outside the entrance to the zoo, groups of families milled about in the early morning sun.

They paid 600 yen each to enter the zoo, but before entering, they stopped the cart and checked to make sure the rabbits were not visible. Then they proceeded through the toll entrance handing their tickets to the gatekeeper as they rolled through with their lunchbox and cart.

"Hey, that was easy!" Toshi exclaimed, as the dolly slid past a row of cherry trees. As they entered the zoo area, a young girl about twelve years old approached them. He stopped the cart.

"Hey, Toshi, what are you doing here?" she asked.

"I'm helping my little sister smuggle her rabbits into the park so her friends can see them," he replied, as his face turned a bright red.

"Why how nice! I didn't know you were such a sweet guy. Can I see them?"

"Just take a quick look until we get to the Panda area," Toshi replied. "We plan to take them out and let Natsumi's friends hold them when no one is looking."

Toshi lifted up the cover to let his friend peek underneath. "Oh, how darling," she cooed. "Can I walk along with you?"

"That would be nice," Toshi answered, blushing.

"Gee, I didn't know you had any girlfriends," Natsumi teased.

"PJ, this is my sister, Natsumi. Don't mind her; she's only ten years old."

"Mind her? I would love to have a sister! I'm an only child. Here, let me help guide the cart," PJ said, as she put her hand on top and followed behind the cart.

From underneath the bamboo, Bilbo and Cody could see a cement structure approaching. They could see a black and white pile of wool slumped sleepily inside a wall of glass. Their dolly slowed to a stop in front of a second glass-covered area. Here, they peeked upward to see a black and white bear with black rings around its eyes lying limp off the shelf's edge.

"Bilbo, that is Ling Ling, a good friend of mine," Sensei said.

The rabbits looked upward at the bear that lay lifelessly on its shelf, as he had for most of the many years Natsumi had been coming to the park.

They waited for the bear to move. They were still waiting for signs of life when a small group of young girls appeared.

"You've got them?" asked the first one to approach. "Let us see!" The children, who had come in the hopes of being able to touch a live rabbit, fawned over the carrier. Toshi lifted up the cover and the children peered in.

"Oh, wow!" they muttered in unison.

"They came all the way from America?" another asked.

"Yes, and look at this one here," Natsumi instructed, as she reached in took Bilbo out. "This is Bilbo Bunny from the book I told you about; he's famous. Here, would you like to hold him first?" Natsumi asked, offering him to her friend to hold.

First one held him, and then another, Toshi's girlfriend PJ, and then the rest. Before long, Ling Ling the panda bear had gotten down from his shelf and wandered over to the commotion. The children held Bilbo up to the glass for him to see.

The panda put his nose on the glass against Bilbo's, and they peered into each other's eyes. A glimmer of light seemed to surround the two for an instant just long enough for all who watched to wonder if it was magic or just a glare from the sun on the glass.

"Hey, there!" Double Delight squealed at the panda.

"Yes, hey there, Ling Ling," Juliet and Cody greeted.

"Hey! I can hear you!" Ling Ling exclaimed. "Where did you come from?" she asked in a series of soft grunts.

"From the farm area of Wheatland, Wisconsin in America," Cody hastily replied.

"Really? I'd like to hear about the outside world. I don't get to see anything like that here," the panda sighed.

They squealed and grunted stories back and forth to one another. Before long, a crowd had gathered in front of the panda area to watch the extraordinary phenomenon. More and more people gathered and it was getting quite out of control when a huge flash of light all but blinded Bilbo.

"Toshi! That was a photographer for The Japan Times," PJ exclaimed. "You better get out of here. You're not supposed to bring pets to the zoo!"

"Oh no! Mother and Father will find out! We better leave quickly," Toshi shouted.

"Bye!" Bilbo called out to Ling Ling.

"We'll be back to visit soon!" Cody shouted back.

The children passed Bilbo from one to another behind their backs until Natsumi was able to hide him under her shirt. She crept slowly away from the crowd, as did Toshi, with the dolly in tow. Soon they had escaped from the crowd as they slipped through the cover of the forest.

"Let's go west toward the Toshogu Shrine, there are less people there!" Toshi ordered. They scurried away quickly, the group of children casually pretending not to be following.

Soon they were all walking down a pathway of massive stone and copper lanterns under the cover of the forest. The group of children gathered around them, and they walked slowly, watching to see if anyone had followed them.

They walked and talked until they reached the Chinese-style Karamon Gate.

"Did you know these lanterns were all gifts to Shogun Tokugowa Leyasu?" Toshi asked PJ.

"Yes, I know a lot about history and legends, also. "Did you know that legend has it that when night falls, the lions on the gate sneak down to the Shinobazu Pond for a drink?" PJ whispered dramatically.

"Maybe we had better get home before the lions get us all!" Toshi warned. "Won't your parents be wondering where you went?"

"Yes, you're right," the children agreed reluctantly.

"Don't worry," Natsumi advised. "I will bring them to school as soon as the government gives me permission, and until then, you can come and see them at my house, upstairs in the attic."

Regretfully, Natsumi bid goodbye to her friends while PJ agreed to walk with Toshi to Benton-do Temple by way of the Shinobazu Pond.

The rest of their walk was uneventful and soon the rabbits were safely tucked away in the attic.

Later that night, Toshi and Natsumi sat quietly in the family room with the TV on. They were playing an electronic pinball game when they overheard a newsflash.

"A strange thing happened at Ueno Zoo today. Ling Ling, the panda bear, was seen being very conversational with a mysterious rabbit that disappeared as this picture was taken. It's been said that the rabbit is magical and has come to bring good health to Ling Ling and Tokyo. Well, so much for the news...we couldn't find a trace of the rabbit or anyone who would admit to having seen the rabbit in question. If anyone has any information on this rabbit, please call the station."

"Natsumi, you'd better call your friends right away and make sure they don't tell the news people," Toshi whispered feverishly.

The Path to the Magic key

~~~~~~~~~~~~~~~~~~~~~~~~~~~~~~~~~~~

Chapter 3

The rabbits were finally settled into their new home and just bedded down for the night. From the attic above the den, Bilbo and Cody lay listening at the heat vent. Below they could see Mr. Hashimoto working at his desk as usual.

They could hear him reading out loud to himself as he made notes. "As the only country to have experienced the devastation caused by the use of atomic bombs, Japan feels obligated to help promote World Peace and disarmament. It is also our hope to establish an honorable position in international affairs, by making a positive contribution. They watched as Mr. Hashimoto prepared an outline, fretting and tapping his pencil after each few words, then scratching out and re-writing new words.

"Dear, will you be much longer?" they heard Mrs. Hashimoto ask from the doorway.

"I'm almost done. Tomorrow when I go to North Korea, I want to make sure I am prepared."

"I hope you don't work too late, my husband," said Mrs. Hashimoto.

"Don't worry, dear. It's a much easier thing that I do than others have to."

Mrs. Hashimoto's footsteps then grew softer and softer and Mr. Hashimoto seemed to finish his writing. He was reflecting on the words when they heard a knock on the front door.

"Who could be calling on him this late?" Cody asked.

"He is the minister of foreign affairs, so it could be anyone," Sensei commented.

"Come in," they could hear Natsumi's dad say as he greeted someone at the door. Soon they could see the two men that Mr. Hashimoto had let into the house.

11

"So you have finished your speech preparation?" one of the men asked.

"Yes, I was just prioritizing the most important points of my speech that we had presented last time in Russia. This time I think it will be easier to understand. I'll make a copy of my outline for you so you know the exact order of my presentation," Mr. Hashimoto instructed.

"I'll be ready to pick you up at five o'clock in the morning," the other man said. Then they watched the men leave as the light shut off behind them.

"I had no idea that he had such an important job," Bilbo said in awe.

"Perhaps it is somehow a part of your future destiny. Natsumi's grandfather gave me good instructions, but we cannot be sure of what any of it means until we follow the path that is laid out before us."

"What do you mean by that, Sensei?"

"Grandfather Riujin instructed me that when a surprise visitor came in the night, we were to visit the Shinto Shrine in Ueno Park. We're to find a secret entranceway at the foot of the small mountain and follow the path until we find a secret scroll."

"Then do you want to go to Ueno Park tonight?" Bilbo asked.

"Well, if world peace is at stake as the grandfather said, we should find out just what is happening as soon as possible," Sensei replied.

"I agree with you," Bilbo answered, as he hopped across the room to the open window. Cody followed close behind.

"I'd been hoping that we could go on another adventure," Cody said, as they both pushed on the screen and then crawled to its edge. As they looked out into the darkness, they could see the top of the next roof, inches away.

"Good luck, Bilbo! Good luck, Cody! You be careful now!" Juliet and Double D called, who sounded just as worried as Mrs. Hashimoto did.

"Well, it's a lot safer than being out in the country back home, no coyotes or anything of that sort," Cody commented, as he hopped across to the other roof and waited for Bilbo.

"That remains to be seen," Sensei whispered from the back of Bilbo's neck.

"What do you mean by that?" Bilbo asked.

"All I'm saying is that Japan is a country full of legends and magic. You just never know what to expect."

"I think that is wonderfully exciting," Cody replied happily. "I love adventures!"

Across the roofs, the rabbits hopped quietly, trying not to wake up the inhabitants below. They found their way down a series of roof tiles, until finally they were standing near the street. Although it was late, there were still many people on the street.

"We could just hop across when no one is looking in this direction," Sensei instructed. "They'll never notice anything so small and quick."

They waited for their opportunity and soon had crossed the Shinobazu highway and were on their way down the path past the boathouse at the Shinobazu Pond. There was a full moon and the park was beautiful. What lights there were seemed to flicker magically, like jewels in the water. They heard pond frogs and the gentle cooing of night birds.

They were passing by Benton-do Temple when they heard a whooshing sound. Something stirred in the air above them. Then a roar and a mournful cry ripped the night air. "Rawh!" It roared above their heads.

"What is that?" Bilbo asked, trembling.

"That is the Golden Dragon," answered Sensei. "Many centuries ago, it was cursed to wander by night, circling over and over, stranded forever within the boundaries of the Shinobazu Pond, a prison from which it can never escape. Don't be afraid, the Golden Dragon is usually a sign of good fortune. It won't hurt you."

They watched as the dragon swooped around and around the small area above, his wings lifelessly drooping and head hung low with eyes cast forlornly downward.

"How sad it looks," Bilbo pondered, as they watched the dragon sweep across the night sky, painfully repeating its flight over and over.

"Well, we have more important business at hand right now. We need to find the clue that Grandfather Riujin has instructed us to obtain. Then we'll know just what it is that is so important," Sensei instructed sternly.

On they hopped, past the pathway of huge lanterns, across the island, deeper into Ueno Park. Overhead, they could see the huge crows that frequented the park, perched in the trees above them. Was it their imagination or did the ravens seem to be following their every move?

They hopped slowly up the steep steps that led to Kannon-do Temple and continued on their way to find the small shrine that was always left open to the public.

"Wait! Let's stop here to wash your paws in the fountain," Sensei said.

"Okay," said Cody and Bilbo, bewildered.

Not knowing why, Cody and Bilbo took a big hop and landed on top of the fountain's edge. Just above them, water poured out of the mouth of a bronze dragon. First Cody washed his paws and then Bilbo.

"Okay, let's get to the shrine," Sensei said. "We will know our destiny once we find the scroll that Grandfather Riujin talked about."

They hopped into a small building where their shrine with the small mountain could be found. As they entered, the fox-like porcelain figurines that guarded the shrine from evil seemed to be watching them. The old scent of incense still clung to the night air.

"Now where would we begin to look for a secret entranceway?" Cody asked.

"You must make a noise to wake the gods and then you'll probably see a sign," Sensei said.

"Okay," Bilbo murmured, as he instinctively thumped his hind legs on the floor. Cody followed his lead and thumped his bunny thump. When nothing happened, they thumped again and again, then listened and waited for a sign.

Finally, a shaft of moonlight cracked through the doorway and shone on the wall of rock. Squinting their eyes, a lit pathway appeared inside the rock wall. Bilbo approached and stretched his paw out to touch the wall. Amazingly, his paw passed right through the rocks. Cautiously, he hopped in and slowly descended into a dimly lit tunnel. Cody followed behind.

"Cody, look at the sides of the tunnel, it's all covered with Japanese writings of some kind!" Bilbo exclaimed. There were beautiful drawings of dragons, samurai warriors, and ancient wars of old. The pictures were drawn very intricately, like the old-fashioned block prints the rabbits had seen hanging in the attic.

"Ah, Cody, I don't like the looks of this," Bilbo commented, as he stopped and stared at the pictures. He had come to pictures of rabbits that looked just like Bilbo and Cody. Behind them were evil raccoon-like dogs with sharp fangs. They seemed to be hunting them.

"Those are tanuki," Sensei explained. "They are a type of dog, native to Japan. They can be either bad or good, but in these pictures, they appear to be evil. In Japanese folklore, they have the power of transforming themselves into living or inanimate objects."

"I wonder why these pictures here are so abstract. They look like they're from that game that Toshi plays with," Bilbo pondered. "It's as if the drawings were to tell of a future event. It would appear that it is to be a warning to us."

As they tunneled on, Cody hopped ahead. "Look at this one! There is Godzilla with a magnificent robe and a crown on his head. See how he commands the tanuki!"

A brighter light drew them forward as they entered a larger chamber of the tunnel. In the middle sat a glass case with gold edges. Inside the glass case sat a yellowed scroll wound up in a red ribbon. A bright golden light seemed to emulate around the case.

"That must be it!" Sensei exclaimed.

"But how do we get it out?"

"It has been waiting especially for you, Bilbo. I think you just open the glass," Sensei answered.

Bilbo approached the golden etched glass case and pressed his paw against the glass. The side of the case fell open and there for the taking was the scroll. He slowly reached in with his paw and slid the scroll forward.

Bilbo sniffed it. It smelled ancient. It smelled important.

"Open it!" Sensei instructed.

Bilbo untied the red ribbon. He caught the curled end of the document on the top edge of the glass and let the scroll fall open.

It seemed to roll open with perfection. A blanket of gold dust showered down and buried itself within their fur coats.

Tied to the end of the scroll was a golden key that fell to the floor with a clunk. This held the scroll open for their viewing.

"It's in Japanese, I can't read it," Bilbo said.

"I can," Sensei chimed in excitedly. "It says, if you have found this scroll, it means that the world is off-balance in favor of evil and it is necessary for you to gather four essential jewels of power in order to restore the power of good.

"At the end of this scroll, you will find the key that you need to open the pathways to the jewels, the first of which you will find at the tomb of Tokugawa Yoshinobu in Yanaka cemetery, but beware of the spirits you find there. Some good, and some that only appear to be good.

"For this, you will now possess the power to discern good from bad. Also, in order to help keep you from harm, you will now have the power of transformation to deceive your enemies.

"Finally, in order for you to accomplish your task and keep your faith, it is imperative that you believe in the possibility of miracles. With these gifts we bid you on your journey...but be wary at all times, lest you lose the true path...

"That is all it says," Sensei commented quietly.

"It seems that the whole world is depending on us to save it," Bilbo reflected.

"I think that's only fitting," Sensei commented. "True power is not achieved by great acts of violence or domination, but by the humblest, tiniest steps, or in this case, hops. I think my forefathers discovered this long ago."

"So it's onto the cemetery to find a new beginning?" Bilbo asked, puzzled.

"Yes, through the past, we construct new beginnings," Sensei affirmed.

"If you know the way, I am ready," Bilbo answered, as he rubbed his bunny chin against the glass case.

"Yes, I'm anxious to see what's next," Cody agreed.

"Take the key from the end of the scroll and tie it around your neck, Bilbo. We will need that when we get to Yoshinobu's tomb site."

Bilbo hopped to the end of the scroll and chewed off the loop of string that attached the key to the scroll, then he placed it on the edge of the stone below and proceeded to dip his head beneath it, wrapping it around his neck.

"On for world peace!" Bilbo cheered. "We are small but we'll be giants in the war against evil!" he exclaimed, as he led the way out of the tunnel.

"Yes, don't anyone underestimate the power of the rabbit!" Cody cheered back, as he picked the scroll up in his mouth.

Then he strode erectly out of the tunnel and into the moonlit night.

"We're on our way!" Sensei cheered. "Turn right toward Toshogu Shrine," he instructed. "Finally, the journey has begun!"

On to Yanaka Cemetary
~~~~~~~~~~~~~~~~~~~~~~~~~~~~~
Chapter 4

Under the cover of night, Bilbo and Cody made their way to Yanaka Cemetery. Following Sensei's instructions, they were soon passing by the lantern-lined pathway that led to Toshogu Shrine.

Piercing the darkness, they heard a deep-throated animal's disgruntled roar cutting eerily through the night air. The hair on their backs stood on end.

"What is that?" Bilbo asked very quietly.

"Don't be frightened, that's just the guard lions from the Toshogu Karamon Gate. Every night they sneak down to the Shinobazu Pond for a drink," Sensei replied. "Just ignore them and head toward Ling Ling's home and we'll soon find our way out of the park."

They followed Sensei's advice and were soon finding their way past a sleeping Ling Ling and her companion. As they passed by, they could see their white fur, as they lay asleep upon the shelves above.

Before long, the museums were behind them and they were entering Yanaka Cemetery. Through the clearing moonlit sky, they could see row upon row of stones and wooden sticks with Japanese writing. The Forest of Japanese Sticks pledged prayers to the quiet inhabitants of the cemetery. Famous physicians, authors, entertainers, and scholars were noted for their accomplishments. They continued searching for Yoshinobu's grave.

"Wait, I think that's it!" Sensei cried out. Ahead, they could see a stone fence protecting an area inside of which sat a large manmade monument. Cody and Bilbo slid under the stone fence and over to the large stone.

"Now what?" Bilbo asked.

19

"I don't really know. Why don't you go around back and look for a keyhole. I don't have any idea where it might be," Sensei answered.

Bilbo and Cody hopped about the stone in what appeared to be a dance-like ritual. They peered up and down, but could not find a keyhole. The moonlight shone on the golden key as it jiggled around Bilbo's neck. It made a click clacking noise on the stones.

"I think that we should look up by the stairs over there," Sensei offered.

Bilbo and Cody crept slowly toward the foundation-like structure, and as they did, a moonbeam shone down on a small keyhole in the stone.

"Quickly, Bilbo, there it is!" Sensei shouted excitedly.

Bilbo strode over to the keyhole and with the key now in his mouth, he pushed it into the hole. All of a sudden, a brick sprung open. Musty air and dust flew into their faces, but under the light of the moonbeam, they could see a bright green jewel glowing profusely, lighting up their faces eerily in the dark. Behind the jewel sat a small dusty scroll. Cody looked at Bilbo and then proceeded to pull out the scroll with his mouth. Then, with his teeth, he pulled the string that bound it closed. The scroll sprung open, just as it did the first time. This scroll also rolled open as if by magic and the gold key turned itself loose and flew to the ground with a loud thud.

"I'll read the scroll," Sensei offered. Bilbo leaned his head down in order for Sensei to get a better look.

"You now possess the first jewel of four, but beware, for all that is evil is watching. Go now to Old Edo Castle and you will find the second. Keep this first one safe underwater until you have all four. Remember the rhyme:

> *Be strong and of good courage,*
> *for now begins the task,*
>
> *But be wary of the fox,*
> *and his ever-changing mask,*

20

*In your heart, you will find the key,
when everything depends.*

*Just don't trust the obvious,
and be careful with whom you make friends.*

Take this ancient packet of Ylang Ylang. Go now and be wary and keep the golden key safe...you will need it to find the three remaining jewels."

They were suddenly interrupted by the whistling sounds of strange, tiger marked, horned creatures flying overhead. "The oni, we must go! The oni seek souls of sinners, so there must already be evil creatures seeking the jewel as we speak!" Sensei shouted. "Quickly, we must go!"

"Bilbo, gather the packet inside the scrolls and take it along with the key!" Sensei shouted as loud as he could. "Cody, you get the gem!"

Cody grabbed the jewel in his mouth as Bilbo slid the golden key around his neck. He then wrapped the package of Ylang Ylang within the other two scrolls that he picked up in his mouth. They hurriedly left the fenced in area that surrounded the tomb. As they sped down the cemetery pathway, they could see the oni flying over the Yoshinobu area, diving downward at even stranger looking creatures.

"The tanuki! We saw them in the cave tunnels! What are they doing?" Cody mumbled with the gem still tight in his mouth.

"They seek the jewel for their evil purposes. All evil will be seeking the jewels now that they are unearthed," Sensei informed them. "Don't worry, I have much wisdom that I have learned over the centuries. I will keep you safe."

As they sped home as fast as they could, they never did feel safe. Everything in the graveyard was following them. Spirits danced gleefully in the night, both good and bad. They rose out of their graves and hovered in the darkness of the night. The crows, which before were resting quietly, were now diving at them. Tanuki followed them as they made their way out of the graveyard toward Ueno Park.

"Cody, close your mouth over the jewel so that it is covered by water!" Sensei instructed, and then shouted, "Fox, shape be fox!"

Cody did close his mouth and soon the tanuki lost them in the dark. At that moment, a cloud passed over the moon and the two rabbits transformed into fox-like shapes in the night. With their larger, newfound disguise, they were soon able to slip down to the Shinobazu Pond, past the golden dragon that flew in circles overhead, and then home. Before long, they had transformed back to their old selves and were soon on the roofs adjacent to their home.

As they crawled through the open window, they heard, "Bilbo, Cody, you're back!" It was Juliet from down below.

"Cody, don't open your mouth!" Sensei shouted. "Go to the fountain and submerge the stone under the water or not one of us will be safe!"

Cody did as Sensei instructed. After Bilbo placed his scroll with Natsumi's fortunes, they got back in the cage with the others. They told them of their adventures and how they now had to travel to Edo Castle.

"Where would that be? Do you know?" Bilbo asked Sensei.

"It is located within the Imperial Palace grounds. There isn't a castle left standing, but the foundation is there. That must be where we're supposed to go."

"Do we hop there?"

"We'll talk it over with Natsumi in the morning. I think we'd better get some sleep," Sensei said as he yawned.

"That's a good idea! We've had a rough night and still more adventures to come," Bilbo said, as they all lay down for the night. He tucked the golden key from the graveyard safely underneath his chin.

Bilbo and Cody were so tired that they didn't even hear Double D and Juliet as they fretted before falling asleep.

"I'm afraid, Juliet."

"So am I, Double D, but we will never be able to convince them to stop. Goodnight, Double D," Juliet said, as she finally fell asleep.

Double D looked up at the moon that shone through the skylight wondering what the next day would bring. She was so tired she didn't even notice the oni flying overhead.

Through the night, the oni swooped in circles over the attic. (An oni is a huge ugly red creature with long nails, horns, and wild hair. They wear tiger skins and search the night sky, in the hope of capturing evil souls.) But what were they doing at Natsumi's house?

A Day at School

~~~~~~~~~~~~~~~~~~~~

Chapter 5

The next morning when they awoke, all seemed safe and cheery again.

"Last night was I dreaming or did we change shape?" Bilbo asked. "I could have sworn that you were a fox."

"And I you," Cody replied.

"It's been foretold. Remember the first scroll? That's an old Japanese trick."

"Trick?" Bilbo queried.

"Yes, a trick of sorts. Once I suggested fox to you, you immediately changed. Next time you can change yourself without my suggestion," Sensei answered, as he stood up on Bilbo's neck to chat with them. "It may be that you will desperately need that ability in the future."

"Oh my gosh!" Juliet exclaimed. "Look at Sensei, he's turned green!"

"What? I've always been white. It must be part of the magic. Ugh, and my skin is all slimy. I hope the grandfather knew what he was doing when he got us involved in this."

"Quiet! Someone is coming!" Cody exclaimed.

Slowly the door opened and Mrs. Hashimoto glided gracefully across the floor. They watched as she checked her silkworm boxes. She then took some processed silk from the table and laid it next to her spinning wheel as if she couldn't wait to spin. She then went to the doorway and called out loudly, "Natsumi, hurry, you will be late for school." Then she opened the window to let in the fresh morning air.

Natsumi finally appeared to remove the rabbits from their cage and place them into her carrier.

"Psst...Bilbo...just so you know...I've spun the key under your neck with a silk string, in case we have a chance to go onto the castle today," Sensei whispered.

"We're going to school to show you to all the other children. I requested permission from the government weeks ago and it's all planned for you to go," Natsumi explained. "You'll have a great time!"

There was nothing they could do but go. They didn't have an opportunity to tell Natsumi about what had happened the night before. Soon, Natsumi had Toshi bringing the carrier down the stairway. Then he and Natsumi placed it onto the trolley and began walking down the sidewalk and through the Shinobazu area, toward Ueno subway station.

"Natsumi, what if the children at school recognize Bilbo from the news report last night?" Toshi asked. "Why don't we put some ashes in his fur so he'll look gray?"

"Uh, excuse me," Bilbo interrupted. "We have something important to tell you."

"What? Did that rabbit talk?" Toshi asked.

"I'm sorry, Toshi. I was going to tell you when I thought I could trust you," Natsumi said, as she stopped walking and brought the trolley to a stop next to a bench in front of the Shinobazu Pond.

"Bilbo, what is it?" Natsumi asked.

"It is important that we talk. Last night we went to your grandfather's favorite Shinto Shrine and found a magic tunnel. Inside the tunnel, we found an ancient scroll that told us that the world has changed in favor of the power of evil. In order to change the power of evil back to good, we were to collect four powerful jewels, the first of which would be in Yanaka Cemetery. We went to Yanaka and collected the first stone. As soon as we collected it, evil creatures seemed to appear from everywhere. Tanuki, oni, even the crows in the park seemed to become evil. We made it safely home and hid the jewel, but now we must go to Edo Castle to get the second jewel."

25

"And not only that, the magic has already begun to happen," Sensei interjected. "My skin has changed to green and it's all scaly. And Bilbo and Cody have the power to change shape."

"All that happened in one night? I know Grandfather said something would happen in the future in which I would be called upon to help find peace for the world, but I never thought it would happen so soon," Natsumi said in disbelief.

"Grandfather told you all these things? How come he didn't tell me anything?" Toshi complained. "And what was that little voice coming from Bilbo's back?"

"I'm sorry. Grandfather said it was destiny for a girl child and a rabbit to bring needed peace to the world," Natsumi answered. It didn't make much sense when he said it, but now I'm beginning to understand. Our Shinto and Buddhist beliefs don't even include evil, but believe in preventing evil acts and promoting a peaceful state. Perhaps it is necessary for us to join forces with the rabbit in order to bring the best out in people around the world. Oh yes, and that little voice is Sensei, a simple silkworm that has lived many years and is here to help us."

"I am hurt that Grandfather didn't think he could trust me. And you, why didn't you tell me they could talk?"

"Toshi, I'm sure your grandfather didn't mean to dishonor you. It is just that this is what is destined," Cody consoled.

"I didn't know if I could trust you to believe me because you still think of me as your silly little sister," Natsumi said apologetically.

"Well, we'd all better get going to school, we can't miss the train. But first, let's disguise Bilbo," Toshi instructed. "I'll go get some ashes from the incense and rub it into his fur."

Toshi was quick to return with the ashes and he began rubbing it gently into Bilbo's fur. "Hatchoo! That makes my nose tickle!" Bilbo exclaimed.

"Hey, what's that key doing wound around your neck?" Toshi asked.

"That's the key we need to open the castle wall," Bilbo explained.

"Wow!" Toshi exclaimed, as he eyeballed the mysterious looking key.

"Bilbo, you look like Cody's brother now," Double D giggled out loud.

"Hatchoo! Phew, that stings, but the ashes may help ward off evil. An excellent idea, Toshi!" Sensei called out from inside Bilbo's fur.

Natsumi brought a cloth cover out of her purse and covered the rabbit's carrier for secrecy. "There now, no one will stop us," Natsumi commented.

"Okay, let's get going!" Toshi urged, as he got up and started pulling the trolley toward the subway station.

Soon they were rolling the trolley down the subway entrance ramp, out of the busy streets. People barely turned their heads at the sight of Natsumi and Toshi and their most remarkable cargo. Since Tokyo has many people journeying in the subways and about with their luggage, the rabbits were hardly noticed. Approaching the train, Toshi and Natsumi each lifted one end of the trolley over the gap to the doorway. Once inside, they rolled it under their seat and sat down.

Everyone on the train was respectfully quiet as usual, although several people stared curiously at the children.

"Toshi, do you think we could visit the Imperial Palace grounds after school today so we could see Edo Castle?" Natsumi asked.

"I will call Mother and see if it's okay," Toshi replied.

Toshi whipped a cell phone out of his pocket and made the call, giving him the necessary permission to be late after school.

"Okay, she said we could be late. We will go to the Imperial Garden after school. Don't be late. I will wait for you at the door, Natsumi," Toshi instructed, as he continued to play a game on his cell phone.

Below, the rabbits could hear Toshi's electronic game making many samurai kills and explosions while the subway train whirred on.

Soon, they reached their destination. Upon exiting the subway station, they were joined by other children dressed in similar blue uniforms, all heading toward their school and into their classrooms.

"I'll see you at three o'clock," Toshi said, as he headed for his own classroom.

Natsumi wheeled her carrier bashfully into the locker room. After rolling the carrier to a safe corner, she removed her shoes and put on her slippers.

"You must wait here until after lunch, then I will show you to the class," she instructed the rabbits.

"Did you bring the rabbits?" asked one of several girls who approached.

"Yes, but the teacher says we must wait until after lunch and cleaning time to see them," Natsumi answered excitedly.

"Can we see them at lunchtime?" one girl persisted, as the group followed a suddenly popular Natsumi into the classroom.

"I'm sure we must wait until one o'clock like our teacher said."

The girls ran off to class, giggling excitedly. Bilbo and the others waited patiently until they again heard the children get their shoes and go outside for lunch. Their cover was taken off and they could then see Natsumi and the others as they cleaned the floors in the hallway across from the locker room. When they were done, Natsumi ran back quickly to get the rabbits.

Natsumi rolled her carrier into the gymnasium for everyone to see. She stood in front of the class and explained that the rabbits were show rabbits from the United States of America and that now they had come to live in Japan.

"Will they be making friends with Japanese rabbits?" asked a young girl.

28

"I don't know any Japanese rabbits for them to be friends with, but I'm sure they could be friends. They are very friendly rabbits," Natsumi answered.

"Can I use them for models for my pinball machine project?" another young boy asked.

"What do you mean?" Natsumi asked nervously.

"I'd like to draw a picture of them to use in my pinball machine design," the boy answered.

"I think that is a very good idea," Natsumi's teacher said. "Maybe our entire class would like to draw some pictures of the rabbits after we're done presenting them here."

"Now, would anyone like to pet their foreheads? It's okay," Natsumi explained.

Soon everyone was crowded around the carrier's top petting the rabbits lovingly.

"These rabbits have quite a long bloodline in America. The number in their ear can be traced to their record of ancestry. It can trace whose parents and grandparents are on their pedigree, along with their show winnings. These rabbits are highly honored," Natsumi bragged.

"Doesn't the tattoo hurt them?"

"Only for a few seconds, it's like an ear piercing," Natsumi explained. "It is necessary in order to keep records, so that the owners don't lose track of their ancestry."

"All right, time is up," the teacher said. "We'll all have to be getting back to our club activities after lunch."

Soon the various classes had returned to their own rooms leaving Natsumi's class to return to theirs with the rabbits.

"Now, whoever would like to draw the rabbits for their pinball machine science projects may," Natsumi's teacher instructed, as she had Natsumi place the rabbit's carrier in the middle of the room on top of the table.

A very popular Natsumi drew all four rabbits' pictures, as did most everyone else. Some of the drawings portrayed the rabbits as samurai combating Godzilla's; some portrayed the rabbits hopping over mountains and lakes and the likes; but Natsumi portrayed the bunnies fighting the dragon at the Shinobazu Pond in Ueno Park. She drew the gold key that dangled from around Bilbo's neck. She also drew a few jewels that sparkled in midair above the dragon. The children worked on their pinball board until the end of the school day.

"Everyone is doing a wonderful job. Your projects show a lot of artistic inspiration. I am very happy with everyone's work here today. You should all be very proud," the teacher praised her class. "Now, you are excused for the day, and don't forget to work on your pinball machine projects at home tonight."

With those last few words of instructions, Natsumi and the others were soon folding up their artwork to work on at home. Natsumi left with her rabbits to the locker room as most of the other children followed.

"I can't believe they're real," Natsumi's friend Aiko said, stroking the rabbits' fur. "They look like cartoon characters."

"Can I follow you to the subway?" she asked right away.

"Well, Toshi and I are taking a walk in the Imperial Garden." Natsumi paused for a minute, thinking whether or not she could trust Aiko.

"We should be home after six o'clock. Why don't you give me a call then?"

"All right, I will."

Natsumi left and waited outside the school door with half of her classmates all cooing about how cute Bilbo and the others were.

"Natsumi, we have to go!" Toshi grunted. "Hurry now or we won't have enough time. We have to get on the Ginza line and get back again before supper. Excuse us, but we have to get going," he said, as he grabbed the trolley's handle and began heading in the direction of the subway.

"Bye!" Natsumi called out to Aiko, as she followed behind the trolley.

Edo Castle and a Dragon's Fury
~~~~~~
Chapter 6

With the cover placed over the rabbits' carrier, they had quickly entered the subway and were whizzing along on their way to Mitsukoshi-mae Station. Upon arriving, they hurriedly exited and took a short cut through the Mitsukoshi Store. The rabbits peeked out from under their trolley. "What visions of pure delight!" Multi-colored desserts and just everything imaginable that one could dream of was there for sale.

"Oh, Toshi, look, can we stop and get one?" Natsumi begged, as she stopped to stare at her favorite dessert.

"No, Natsumi, some other time. Let's get going. It's a long walk to the castle. We'll have to take the JR line back; it is a little closer for us."

After a long tiring walk, they were outside the Imperial Palace moat and through its entrance gateway. Drawing little attention to their covered trolley, they safely made their way in.

"Phew! This seems to be working quite nicely. I don't know what Dad would do to me if he found out what we were up to," Toshi said.

"What do you mean?"

"I just told Mom that we were going to Aiko's house after school to show her the rabbits. We still have to get home as soon as possible for supper so that they don't find out," Toshi explained.

"Uh oh, I told Aiko to call me after six o'clock. We better get home or Mom will find out we weren't at Aiko's house," Natsumi quipped, as they hurriedly wheeled past the extraordinarily groomed garden area and made their way toward the old castle walls. "That leaves us no time for error."

Toshi pulled the trolley as quickly as he could until they reached the bottom of the old Edo Castle foundation and then stopped.

31

"What do we do now? How do we know where the key goes?" Bilbo asked out loud.

"Well, the jewel has been waiting here for centuries and no one's found it. There must be something special about the key. Hold the key up to the sunlight and see if anything happens," Sensei instructed.

Bilbo twisted his neck and grabbed the key with his mouth, turning it up toward the sun. The sun shown on the key. A beam of light bounced off of it, directing itself toward a spot on a faraway moat wall. The light bounced back toward the opposite side of the castle foundation wall from which they were standing. Eerily enough they could hear a few twangs of notes emanating from the sunlit air as if a magical harp had been plucked.

"That must be a sign," commented Sensei. "Natsumi, let Bilbo out. It must be he who uses the key."

Natsumi opened the carrier and they all followed as he scurried to the spot from which the beam of light was directed. Cautiously, Bilbo gazed quickly to see if anyone was looking as he then hopped up to the wall and placed the key into the hole, which was now clearly obvious within the glowing spot. He turned the key and the stone slowly grated out of its century's old spot, crumbling the mortar edges that held it in place. When the billow of mortar dust cleared, they could see a red jewel setting upon the top of a ledge. They watched as a magic scroll unrolled itself into the daylight air.

"Wow!" Toshi exclaimed. "It says, Now you have the second of four...against evil you must have four score...so go on to find number three at Toshogu Shrine where once was Kansei. Remember the clue words that compose the rhyme:

It is decreed that peace shall be brought to the world,
When and where its treasures must be unfurled,
When the dragon and the rabbit, they join forces,
Then good and evil will change their courses.

Take this packet of Exotic Basil. It is one of the ingredients that you will need at the end of your journey."

"Okay, roll up the packet of herbs in the scroll, Natsumi," Bilbo instructed. "We'll save everything...until we figure out the clues."

Natsumi picked up the packet of Basil and the scroll and put them into her pocket. She then picked up the key and tucked it back under Bilbo's neck. Bilbo picked up the gem stone off the ledge and quickly closed his mouth over it.

"Hurry, let's get on our way in case the presence of the gem is felt by evil beings," Sensei warned.

Bilbo hopped back over to the carrier and leapt back in, watching Natsumi as she carefully closed the top and covered it. Toshi picked up the handle to the trolley and proceeded to pull it through the lush green garden path that led back to the imperial garden with Natsumi following behind. Soon they had reached the gardens and they paused to catch a glimpse of the fall flowers. Precision trimmed bushes surrounded a multitude of colorful flowers, forming a kind of maze. The rabbits strained to see through their cover. They watched as a couple of garden-tenders clipped away individual flowers that had started to wilt.

"I've never seen anything so beautiful in my life," Double D commented. "How fortunate we are to be in such a grand country."

Bilbo looked down at his reflection in a pool of water surrounded by flowers. He was admiring the serenity when he noticed Sensei sticking his head out from under his fur. "Oh my, Sensei," he said, as he stuck the gem in the side of his mouth. "You have changed again. You have red trim all over. Look at your reflection!"

Sensei and the others all looked. It was true. A red line ran from the top of his forehead all the way to the end of his tail. He now had red eyebrows and red feelers protruding out on either side of his nose.

"I've never seen a silkworm like that before. There must be some mistake," Toshi commented. "He must not have been a true silk worm."

"Actually, I have had thoughts of flying over the years that almost seem like dreams from long ago," Sensei replied.

"Everyone act normal and don't look up. I just saw a couple of men in uniform patrolling the gardens as if they were looking for something," Toshi said. "I want to get out of here quickly."

Toshi picked up the handle of the trolley and tried to act nonchalant.

"I think we better get going, Natsumi. Mother will have our heads if we are late for supper."

"All right, Toshi, but I do so love the flowers; just let me pick up those two chrysanthemum leaves that have fallen out of the tender's basket."

Natsumi stooped to pick up the petals and as she did, she peeked to see a uniformed man to her right.

"Okay, Toshi, let's go."

Very slowly, Toshi pulled the trolley ahead.

"Just a moment, son," Toshi heard the man call out.

"Oh no, we're going to get in trouble," Natsumi fretted. "Dad might be embarrassed by his government co-workers if they find out we've been bringing the rabbits out where they don't belong."

The man proceeded to approach them.

"Maybe he won't ask what's under here," Juliet whispered.

"Cross your paws for luck," Cody whispered back.

"What have you got there in the cart," the man asked.

"My sister brought this cart to school today with permission and we were visiting the gardens before we went home," Toshi replied.

The man looked suspiciously at the cart and then at Natsumi. Natsumi tried to look young and innocent.

"You both know this can't be the direct way home. What would your parents say?"

"I'm afraid we might be late for supper. We were just stopping for a moment to admire the flowers. We wanted to see them before they all wilted," Toshi answered.

"You're lucky I don't stop you and call your parents. Lucky for you we are looking for some bad men that were seen prying out a stone from the castle wall a moment ago. You had better thank your luck and hurry on your way home."

"We certainly will, sir!" Toshi said obediently. "Come now, Natsumi, no more child-play, we must go directly home!"

"Yes, brother."

With a deep sigh of relief, Toshi pulled forward and didn't say a word until they were out of the palace gates.

"Thank goodness. I thought he was going to call Mom and Dad!" Toshi lamented.

"As well as I," Natsumi whined.

Almost running now, they proceeded past the garden fountain as they made their way quickly past the police box and the bank, to Tokyo Station, where they could take the JR train to Ueno. Toshi pulled up to the token booths and purchased the correct fares to Ueno Park, handing Natsumi her own.

"Don't say a word, Natsumi, not the whole way home," Toshi said sternly.

Then Toshi walked quickly through the toll booths where he pushed through the bars as he simultaneously put in his tickets and pulled his luggage ahead, out of the way of the busy people following him. Natsumi did the same and followed her stern brother as he pulled the cart directly off the platform and into the JR train door opening. He found that they had to stand up and hold onto a rope overhead because the traffic was heavy, which was usual this time of day. The train was filled with people on their way home from work or from a busy day of shopping. There should be no problem now, Toshi thought to himself. The trains are usually run on time, like clockwork. He felt relieved that they were on their way home, although he hoped no one would ask what was under the shrine-like cover. About half an hour later, they were exiting at JR Ueno Station. They hurried back down the busy streets and around the corner to their shortcut through Ueno Park. It was a long way to walk, but a typical day in Tokyo.

It was now 5:00 P.M. and it was beginning to get very dark as they pulled their cart past the Shinobazu Pond. They could see the translucent silhouette of the dragon flying overhead. The sun cast blue and orange colors onto it, against the background of an almost full moon rising.

"What a beautiful sight!" Bilbo commented.

All of a sudden, the dragon lunged down at the little cart.

"Oh, Buddha! What was that!" Toshi exclaimed, as he ran with the cart as fast as he could.

"Keep your mouth closed, Bilbo," Sensei ordered. "The dragon senses your jewel. Dragons are notorious for their love of jewels!

"Toshi! The dragon can't get us once we're out of the pond area. Run as fast as you can."

Toshi ran as quick as he could, pulling the cart down the path past Benton-do Temple toward the back exiting Shinobazu-dori. They were almost out of the Shinobazu area when the dragon made a second swoop at the cart. As he did, his claws caught the top of the cover and pulled it up and away. Toshi looked back and could see the carrier was still there, and that's all that mattered.

Soon they had reached Shinobazu-dori Avenue, safely out of the boundaries of the Shinobazu Pond. When they arrived home, Toshi handed the cart to Natsumi.

"Natsumi, you bring them in and put them away. I'm going to try and see if the dragon dropped the cover. We're probably going to need that again."

"All right, Toshi, but please be careful!" Natsumi begged.

Toshi walked off into the dusk. When he returned to the pond area, he could see the dragon still holding the cover in his claws as he flew over the pond, his silhouette making a strange sight against the high-rise buildings in the background. Toshi watched and waited to see if the dragon might drop it. He sat and waited in the twilight outside of Benton-do Temple. The familiar stone lanterns that lined the walkway gave him something to blend into. Toshi respected the lanterns. He knew that in the past, the many lanterns were given to the emperors as gifts. In Ueno Park alone there had to be at least 100 of them and perhaps thousands of them across Japan. Also, the trees hid Toshi from the prying eyes of the dragon. He was not alone though. There were several homeless men sleeping on the benches, as is so often the case in Ueno Park. Yet Toshi knew he was quite safe. There was not much chance of crime due to the fact that crime is not an honorable thing in Japan. Toshi knew these men probably lost their jobs and were probably too proud to accept charity. He was thinking these salarymen were similar to fallen Samurai warriors, the difference being, they lost their fight in the job world.

Now Toshi noticed the dragon descending from the sky. It held out its claws as if braking for a landing and landed on the opposite side of the shore, in the weeds. It clawed at Toshi's cover, sniffing, as if to sniff out the jewel. Finding nothing, it let out a piercing roar and blew fire out of its mouth. Then with one last sad cry, it dove under the water. Toshi watched until the water grew still. All this time, the men on the bench never stirred. Toshi thought that was strange, but decided to go get the cover back, which lay submerged on top of the grassy weeds.

Upon reaching the other side of the pond, Toshi found a long stick and used it to drag the cover back to shore. He wondered if that was where the dragon might live; it was the only spot shallow enough for weeds to grow. Perhaps the dragon hid its jewels there? Where was he now? He quickly grabbed the torn cover and then sprinted for home.

Arriving home, he removed his shoes in the entranceway, stowed the much soiled cover in his bedroom, and then joined the family for supper. Toshi nodded at Natsumi to indicate he had found the cover.

"Natsumi, how was school today? Did the children like the rabbits?" Mrs. Hashimoto asked.

"Oh yes, very much. In fact, most of them added them to their pictures they are drawing for their pinball machine projects."

"And did you have fun at Aiko's?" her father asked.

"Yes," Natsumi answered while crossing her fingers under the table.

"Aiko is so excited, she wants to call me after supper and maybe visit with them again this evening," Natsumi said, as she scooped up more rice and vegetables.

"I'm afraid you will have to wait until this weekend. It is too late now and your father has business friends coming over tonight," Mother instructed.

Natsumi saw that it was almost 6:00 now. She was prepared to run to the phone if it should ring, which it did.

"No, Natsumi, your father is expecting a call," Mother said, as she intercepted Natsumi on her way to the phone.

"Hello? Aiko? Yes, she's right here," Mrs. Hashimoto replied.

"Now don't speak very long. Your father is waiting for a call," she said, handing the phone to Natsumi.

"Hi, Aiko! No, my mom said that we have to wait until this weekend. I'm sorry, but we will have a great time then. Mother said you could stay overnight and Jimmy could stay in Toshi's room if he comes. All right. We'll talk tomorrow at school."

Natsumi hung up the phone and helped her mother clear the dishes. Her father retired to his office where he received his phone call.

After Natsumi and Toshi had finished helping their mother clean up, they were allowed to go up to the attic and play with the rabbits.

When Natsumi and Toshi arrived upstairs, the rabbits were already in a deep discussion.

"We were talking about our plans on how to go to Toshogu Shrine. It is too dangerous for any of us to go at night because of the dragon," Bilbo said.

Natsumi removed the scroll from her pocket. "Where should we keep this?" she asked.

"We put the other one where you keep your fortune, behind the stone in the bonsai garden," Cody informed her.

"That makes two, and two to go!" Bilbo said. "Now how do we go to Toshogu Shrine?"

"We could go on our way back from school one day," Toshi offered.

"No, it must be Bilbo that uses the key for it to work," Sensei replied.

"Well then, I guess we have to wait for the weekend," Toshi agreed.

"How about Saturday?" Toshi suggested.

"That would be good," answered Natsumi. "I'll have to tell Aiko that they can come over later in the day on Saturday."

"Oh, let me get the carrier cover and see what damage is done to it," Toshi said, leaving the room.

He returned with the cover in his hands. Holding it up to the light, they could see that not only was it torn to shreds, but also thoroughly coated with a sparkling mixture of gooey slime and a dazzling dusty substance.

"Eww, what is that?" Natsumi asked.

"Dragon dust! Fantastic! We just might need that to attract a dragon for one reason or another," Sensei exclaimed. "Good going, Toshi! Scrape off as much as you can and save it somewhere where your mother won't find it. That is one of the best things you could have found!"

"Why is it so important?" Toshi asked.

"Dragon dust can be used for many things. It can be used for luring or taming dragons. It can also be used for invisibility if it is sprinkled on oneself."

"Wow, I can see how the power of invisibility could be quite useful to us right now!" Bilbo exclaimed.

They were interrupted by the sound of strangers' voices rising up through the heating vent.

"Listen!" Sensei ordered.

They all pierced their lips closed and strained to hear what they could.

"It did not go as well as we planned. I'm afraid that they will be proceeding with their nuclear development," said one masculine voice.

Sensei whispered in Bilbo's ear to get out of the cage and see what they could at the heating vent.

Getting out, Bilbo hopped quietly past Natsumi and Toshi to the vent and strained his neck downward to see what he could. Toshi and Natsumi also slipped quietly to the vent to watch.

They could see two men besides their father. The large one was the man who had just spoken.

They heard the slighter man say, "Oh, I would not be concerned. I feel that the peace efforts are coming along well. There is no need for alarm."

"If you're wrong, the world could be at great risk," their father answered.

"No, I am quite sure. Our agents across the world are reporting that all arms are being reduced in accordance and in compliance with the agreements," the thin man said.

"Then we will go on as planned and not alert our allies of any insurgence?" their father asked.

"It is the only thing we can be sure of," the larger man agreed.

"To be sure, everything is going well," the thin man reassured.

"All right, we will report tomorrow what we have discussed, that all is well in our peace keeping efforts and that after making lengthy searches, we find no reason to doubt that the arms reduction is in place in all locations," their father agreed. "Now we will meet tomorrow and report these findings. I thank you both for coming."

The two men shook their father's hand and walked out with him. From in the attic, Bilbo and the others could hear the door closing behind them.

"Did you see what I saw?" Sensei asked.

"That the thin man was really a white fox in disguise?" Bilbo questioned.

"Yes! You have the gift of seeing one's true self. You saw behind his disguise!" Sensei answered.

"I didn't see a fox," Toshi frowned.

"Nor I," Natsumi agreed.

"That is why we must all stay together to complete our task. We each have gifts we can share to complete the task," Sensei informed. "And it seems ever more important that we must get on with our task. A white fox foretells calamity. A fox can pretend to be human in order to lead men astray. They have the ability to change shape, but their faces remain fox-like. Legends tell of how they can hypnotize people and lead them into perilous situations."

"So then, it's planned for Saturday morning?" Toshi asked.

"Yes!" the others agreed.

Natsumi then helped Bilbo back into his cage for the night and she and Toshi bade their goodnights.

They turned off the light as they left the room.

"Bilbo? You will try to be careful won't you?" Double D asked with a quivering voice.

"Yes, I will. When all this business is done, we'll all go out on the town and see Tokyo."

41

"And you, Cody, you must be careful too," Juliet pleaded.

"Yes, I will. We will soon be celebrating and putting this all behind us."

"All right you two, let's get some sleep!" Juliet and Double D sang their rabbit lullaby and with that, they all settled down for the night and dreamt of their adventures that day.

Under the light of the skylight, they were protected for now from the dark shadows that flew ominously overhead.

Toshogu Shrine
~~~~~~~~~~~~~~~~~~~
Chapter 7

Over the next few days, Natsumi continued to work on her pinball machine project up in the attic each night after school. Toshi scraped all the dragon dust he could gather off of the carrier cover and put it in a quart jar that he hid away.

Early Saturday morning, Toshi and Natsumi came to the attic to plan their trip to Toshogu.

"Toshi, how will we bring Bilbo without the carrier cover? How will we hide it? We can't bring it back into Ueno Park without a cover or something. For one thing, pets aren't allowed and another thing is that people might recognize Bilbo from his visit to Ling Ling," Natsumi fretted.

"I've already thought about it. We could bring him in our backpack," Toshi replied.

"That sounds like an excellent idea," Sensei chirped.

"What about me? I always go with Bilbo," Cody pleaded.

"All right, we'll each carry a backpack," Toshi agreed, "but no more!"

"Sorry, Double D and Juliet, you'll have to stay home and watch the jewels," Natsumi consoled.

"We understand," they answered somewhat dismayed at not being able to go to the park, "but just what can we do if something is after the jewels?"

"The main thing is that they just need to stay under water, and nothing should be aware of their presence," Sensei instructed. The other thing we must all watch is that Mrs. Hashimoto does not discover the scrolls and herb packets."

"All right, we will do what we must," Double D affirmed. "You all be careful though!"

43

It was decided that Toshi would put Bilbo in his backpack, just in case he needed to do any fast running or fighting off of any ominous dragons or such. Before long, Bilbo was in Toshi's backpack, Cody was in Natsumi's, and they were happily out the door.

They crossed Shinobazu-dori Avenue and took the back entrance to the pond area. Walking past Benton-do Shrine through the Shinobazu area, everything seemed calm enough, not anything like the night they had returned from Edo Castle. It was a bright sunny day and they hoped not to have any problems. The only problem that could arise was that there might be too many people in order to accomplish what they needed to do.

Bilbo and Cody could smell the burning incense as they passed the shrine and made the long walk down the lantern-lined path that bridged the little island to the land. They could hear waterfowl and frogs outside their backpacks and they pictured how fine the pond must look on such a bright sunny day.

"Natsumi, might you make a peephole for us?" Bilbo asked.

"Oh, I'm sorry. We could open the zipper a little bit, but please keep your head in so no one sees you," Natsumi said. They paused as they exited the path of lanterns in a public concession area.

Natsumi zipped opened Toshi's bag a bit and then she turned around while Toshi unzipped hers a little.

They could see flower exhibits on display on one side and an ancient vendor's cart selling Japanese food on the other. There were many people in this area of the park already, as this was a foot crossroads of sorts for people getting to and from various areas, such as JR Station and to the airport subway station.

They crossed Zoo-dori Avenue and took a flight of stairs that led up through a set of red tori gates. Upon reaching the top of the hill, they passed around Gojo Shrine near where Bilbo and Cody began their adventure in the tanuki tunnel. Now being uphill, Toshi decided to take the path that led past the Great Buddhist Pagoda, past the Statue of Prince Komatsu, and finally, past the five story pagoda to the entrance path to Toshogu.

Bilbo and Cody enjoyed the lengthy lantern-lined pathway to Toshogu Shrine. The trees arched over the path reminding them of home, much like Ueno Park, but here it seemed more dense and mysterious. Above them, they could hear the crows squawking loudly but with a tropical sound unfamiliar to the rabbits. As they finally entered the gateway, Bilbo and Cody noticed the dragons on the Karamon Gate entranceway, the dragons that supposedly go down to the Shinobazu Pond at night to get a drink, although Toshi and Natsumi had told them that that was just a legend.

They watched while Natsumi and Toshi washed their hands in the fancy water trough. Again, they sensed more incense coming from in front of the shrine.

Then their eyes caught sight of the shrine. What a beautiful sight! Vibrant red with dragon carvings decorated up above and multicolored lattice joined beams on top. There was real gold painted trim and details of many different colors.

They waited while Natsumi bought a fortune. She also bought a prayer tablet, wrote a wish on it, and brought it with her to place inside the temple. Then they watched as she and Toshi proceeded to the back entranceway. As they made their way, they noticed that a palace-like wall surrounded the shrine, all with the same elaborate coloring.

Approaching the back entrance, they noticed a set of golden doors where they weren't allowed in. This was where Toshi and Natsumi removed their shoes outside and placed them on a wooden shelf. They then went up a few stairs into what Bilbo thought was the main shrine area. Here he could see two ominous lion-type figures with horns protruding from their heads, guarding a stairway that led up to where there was a kneeling pad in front of a set of golden panels. Inside the gold panels, he imagined there must be some kind of idol hidden away.

Bilbo watched as Natsumi hung her wooden tablet to the side of the lions. The shrine was very ornate inside. There were two Japanese statues standing on either side of the stairs leading up to the golden panels. Natsumi and Toshi nonchalantly looked about to see if anyone was watching.

Seeing no other people about, Toshi asked out loud, "What now?"

"Bilbo needs to hold the key up out of the sack and see if it gives a sign. I would think that this would be the most likely place for the jewel to be found," Sensei replied. "Toshi, let Bilbo and Cody get down so Bilbo can get his key out. Cody or someone will have to help carry the scroll and the jewel. I think it's better if the rabbits go; they won't be noticed as much if someone catches us in the act."

Toshi and Natsumi removed their backpacks and set them on the floor off to the side of the lion statues. Bilbo held the key up. A gold beam of light immediately found its way, first to the lion's eyes whereupon they heard a chiming sound and then they watched as the beam of light held steady on the panel door. The door opened magically revealing a golden Buddha-like statue inside.

"Bilbo, you're going to have to go into the sacred area," Sensei instructed.

"Okay, here we go," Bilbo said, as he and Cody hopped up the shiny black stairway leading through the gold paneled doorway. As they slipped through the door, the others watched as the door closed behind them.

Once inside, Bilbo stood on his hind legs and raised the key in the air again. The gold beam emanated against the golden back wall. They hopped to the wall and saw that the beam bounced back again onto the back of the base of the idol. They then hopped over to the base and pointed the key directly at it. They could hear chiming sounds above as a secret drawer creaked slowly open at the base of the idol, a haze of dust billowing out. Hopping over, they could then see a blue gem and another scroll with a small satchel inside the drawer.

"Just pick up the scroll and satchel and bring them back with the jewel to read later. I'm fearful that we may be interrupted," Sensei said, sounding worried.

46

"Okay, I think we've learned our lesson about that gem," Bilbo said obediently, as he picked up the gem in his mouth and covered it over tightly.

Cody followed, picking up the other items with his teeth, while checking to see if anything else was inside the drawer. "All right, I don't see anything else in there," Cody confirmed.

The two took one last look around at the ornately beautiful golden vault. It seemed so sacred, they could only dream of what history it would tell if it could speak. Then they proceeded back to the gold paneled door from whence they had entered and Bilbo again held up the golden key. Again, the panel magically opened and they could see Toshi and Natsumi waiting for them. They quickly hopped down the stairway to the waiting backpacks and were stuffed in, closed up, and raised back up to Toshi and Natsumi's backs. Bilbo and Cody watched as they entered the other main hallway that they would have entered in if they had come in the front entranceway. There were beautiful wood-carved dragons, stunning murals of dragons on the walls, ornate carvings in the woodwork, and gold filigree in the tiles of ancient wood in the ornately decorated ceiling. Also, brass-plated artworks were applied to the ceiling's edges. They couldn't help but feel a sense of wonder at the beautifully detailed work and the ancientness of the building that was dedicated to Tokugawa Leyasu in 1651, the last Shogunate line in Japan.

They then proceeded out of the building onto the balcony-like walkway, taking a little time to enjoy themselves, since all seemed to be going so well.

"Look," Toshi said, "look at the outside of the building!"

Natsumi rested for a minute against the veranda that surrounded the building and looked upward. Bilbo and Cody gazed upward also. They could see intricate well-crafted carvings of birds, flowers, more dragons, ornately painted lattice like braided woodwork, and more and more gold work. They then looked back toward the Chinese-styled Karamon Gate that they had come through and again noticed the dragon figurines staring back at them. They did seem a little threatening, although it did feel so grand inside the shrine walls that Bilbo and the others would have liked to stay. They all felt as if they could be taken back in time at any moment on a magic carpet ride. After all, hadn't just about everything else happened to them in the past few days?

Too late; now more people were coming through the building behind them.

Toshi nodded at Natsumi to leave and proceeded around the terrace to the back of the building again, back to where they had entered. Here they sat down while they put their shoes on and made their way back through the Karamon gateway, and back down the path that led through the lantern and tree-lined pathway.

"Ah, that seemed easy," Toshi commented. "There were no problems?"

"None at all," Cody answered. "Sensei instructed us not to open the scroll until we got home and stuck the gem under water."

"I guess we had better go straight home then, unless we can immerse Bilbo underwater," Natsumi giggled.

As they walked down the pathway, Bilbo and Cody noticed that the crows were acting a bit peculiar. They all seemed to be glaring at them. Then all of a sudden, they started diving at Toshi. Toshi began to run with Natsumi running after, looking for a stick or something to knock them off.

"There are no sticks to be found in the temple area," Natsumi panicked. "Try to run as fast as you can and I will try to run into the forest and find one to fight them off."

"Forget it, I'm coming with you!" Toshi screamed, as he fought off the crows.

"Ah, here's one," Natsumi said, as she ripped a piece of fencing off of a storage area in the forest.

"Take that you brutes!" Natsumi shouted, as she struck at the birds.

"Caw, caw," the birds threatened, as they slowly gave up.

Toshi kept running all the way back, not only to avoid more crows, but also because they were causing a spectacle as all the people and security guards near the park monorail that they were racing by began to watch.

"These gems better be worth the trouble," Toshi complained, as he made it to the edge of a hill that led down past Ueno Seiyoken Grill and took a path down the hill. Still not safe, the crows followed them all the way to the Shinobazu Pond where they finally let up.

"Oh, Toshi, look at yourself!" Natsumi exclaimed.

Toshi was quite a sight, scratched and bloodied by the birds' claw marks.

"We need to clean you up before Mother sees you. I have some tissue in my backpack. I could try blotting you with some water from the fountain at Benton-do Shrine," Natsumi offered.

"Good idea," Toshi responded.

Soon they were sitting at the lantern-lined pathway in front of Benton-do shrine. Toshi sat down and waited for Natsumi to come back with the wet Kleenex.

"Ah, that's better," Toshi sighed.

"Well, it could have been a lot worse," Sensei commented from within the backpack.

"I can't wait to get home and read the scroll," Cody said excitedly.

Arriving back home, they rushed up to the attic to immerse the gem under the fountain water with the others. Bilbo spat it out under the water.

"There, now let's see what the scroll says!"

Toshi and Natsumi sat down on the floor with their legs crossed, as Cody and Bilbo and then Juliet and Double Delight completed a small circle. Natsumi helped hold down the scroll while they all strained to read.

The last ingredient is one you must know in your heart.
You must go where bamboo grows.
Where once he was, he did depart,
Where your friends might hear a babbling brook.
It's where in the end; all was took.
There you must find the dragon bone,
For this can take you back to another's home.
To find the gem that was lost but now is found,
For you need all four, to bring to the waters on the
* palace grounds.*

"All right, what can it all mean?" Toshi asked, puzzled.

"It says that we need to go somewhere, but it doesn't say exactly where, it's a riddle," Sensei said.

"Why does it give us a riddle? The scrolls were always clear before," Bilbo said.

"I think that it is to guard evil from decoding any of this and being able to stop it or use it for its own gain," Sensei said. "I think it has always been Natsumi's special destiny, ordained before she was even born."

"The bamboo, the babbling brook, and the place where once he was, he did depart. I think that that is Kamakura, where Grandfather once took me," Natsumi said, seeming quite sure of herself.

"So do we just need to go to Kamakura and then figure out where once we get there, or do you know exactly where to go?" Toshi asked.

"The bamboo is near Hokokuji Temple. There is a tea garden that Grandfather and I used to go to very often, and near there is a babbling brook. That must be where it means; I just have a strong feeling about it. There are old incinerator vaults built into the hills there.

'Where in the end, it is where all was took,' I think that that could mean the Yagura Cave that is close to the brook."

"For this can take you back to another's home, to find the gem that was lost but now is found," Double Delight and Juliet recited in unison.

"Could that mean we are to travel back home to retrieve the prism stone from the woodhogs?" asked Bilbo.

There was quiet in the room while they all re-read the rhyme and pondered.

"What prism?" Toshi asked.

"There was a prism found near the water back home in America. It was found by a forest creature, a flying woodhog, something like a groundhog but it likes to chew wood," explained Bilbo. "This flying woodhog, whose name is Windwalker, figured the jewel could be used for good things and he kept it safe from the other evil woodhogs who were always after it. But then one day, the evil woodhogs kidnapped one of my first born kits, Binky, and held him captive in exchange for the prism. There was a struggle which ended up with the evil woodhogs keeping the prism."

"That means we will have to fight to get it back?" Toshi asked.

"With your help, there should be no problem tricking the forest creatures," Sensei encouraged. "No one ever said that saving the world was going to be easy."

"Then our next plan is to go to that place called Kamakura?" Cody asked.

"I have been asking Mother and Father if we could go there for a long time," Natsumi offered. "Maybe if I'm more persistent they will let us go."

"Aiko is coming over soon, you could talk to Mother about it then," Toshi suggested.

"That sounds like a good plan," Natsumi agreed. "Maybe we could try for tomorrow then?" Natsumi asked, as she looked inside the satchel marked Frankincense & Myrrh and then put it away with the others. "Nothing unusual in there."

"Do you think we could review the other two scrolls?" Toshi asked Bilbo and Cody.

"Oh yes, good idea," Cody said, as he hopped and got them. Spreading out the other two scrolls, they all read.

> *Be strong and of good courage, for now begins the task,*
> *But be wary of the fox, and his ever-changing mask.*
> *In your heart, you will find the key,*
> *when everything depends,*
> *Just don't trust the obvious,*
> *and be careful with whom you make friends.*

> *It is decreed that peace shall be brought to the world,*
> *When and where its treasures must be unfurled.*
> *When the dragon and the rabbit, they join forces,*
> *Then good and evil will change their courses.*

> *The last ingredient is one you must know in your heart.*
> *You must go where bamboo grows.*
> *Where once he was, he did depart,*
> *Where your friends might hear a babbling brook.*
> *It's where in the end; all was took.*
> *There you must find the dragon bone,*
> *For this can take you back to another's home.*
> *To find the gem that was lost but now is found,*
> *For you need all four, to bring to the waters on the*
> *palace grounds.*

"When we get the next clue, we should know where the waters on the palace grounds means," Sensei said. "It could mean the Shinobazu Pond or the Grand Fountain that is built where the original Kanei-ji Temple used to be before it was destroyed in the Shogun wars.

"Natsumi! Aiko and Jimmy are here!" Mrs. Hashimoto called up the stairs.

A Trip To Ameyayokocho

~~~~~~~~~~~~~~~~~~~~~~~~~~~~~~~~

Chapter 8

"I'll put the scrolls away while you go get them," Toshi ordered.

When Natsumi came back up the stairs, Toshi was sitting with Bilbo in his lap and the other rabbits were sitting in their cages as if nothing much was happening.

"Toshi, this is Aiko's brother, Jimmy," Natsumi said, as she introduced the two. "That is Bilbo in Toshi's lap. This is Cody," she said, as she picked up Cody and handed him to Jimmy. "And this is Juliet," she said, handing her to Aiko. "This is Double Delight," she said, as she picked her up and held her close. "We could let them hop around," she suggested, as she set Double Delight on the floor.

They giggled as they watched the rabbits hop about the room, investigating everything.

"Do you want to start working on our pinball projects now?" Natsumi asked.

"I was hoping before that we could go to the arcade and play games for a while," Aiko replied.

"That sounds great! We could get ideas from the games there," Natsumi responded. "Let's go talk to my mother and let her know. I have something else I want to talk to her about anyway."

"Jimmy, we're going downstairs. We'll be right back," Aiko told her brother who was busy playing samurai rabbits with Cody, Bilbo, and Toshi.

After putting Juliet and Double Delight away in the cage, the two girls went downstairs to find Mrs. Hashimoto in the kitchen.

"Mother, we'd all like to go to the game arcade before we work on our pinball projects so we can get ideas. Is that all right?"

"Just an hour would be okay. I don't want you there more than that," Natsumi's mom answered while she was preparing a dish for lunch.

"There's something else, Mother. Toshi and I were hoping we could go see Grandmother tomorrow. We have been missing her so much...and I was hoping to visit Hokuku-ji and have tea there in the garden where Grandfather used to take me," Natsumi pleaded. "I used to feel so close to him there under the leaves of the bamboo and the trickling stream."

"Well, tomorrow we have plans, but next weekend would be good. I will call Grandmother and let her know we'd like to come. It would be good for her."

"Great! I can't wait!" Natsumi exclaimed, as she kissed her mother on the cheek. Then she and Aiko turned and ran back up the stairs to tell Toshi and Jimmy.

"All right! Are you two ready to go?" Aiko shouted.

"Sure. We decided to bring Bilbo and Cody in the backpacks to show our friends at the arcade," Toshi explained.

"We've got them packed and ready to go," Jimmy said, as he tugged on his backpack.

"Oh. Well, I guess if you don't mind carrying them. Let's go!" Natsumi squealed excitedly, as she started walking toward the stairs.

The four happily made their way across Shinobazu-dori Avenue, across the Shinobazu Pond path that led past Benton-do Shrine, and then Zoo-dori Avenue to Ameya Yokocho Avenue.

"Wait a minute, could we walk through Ameyayokocho just a little? I need to buy my mom a gift for her birthday," Aiko explained.

"All right, but we've only got an hour that we're allowed to go to the arcade," Natsumi reminded Aiko.

From within their backpacks, Bilbo and Cody could see many brightly colored signs with cheery Japanese writing. They could only wonder what wonderful things the signs offered potential customers in the unique and diverse shopping area. They saw many displays of Japanese dinners, exotic fruits like watermelon and pineapple on a stick. There were also plenty of fresh caught seafood displays. Bilbo and Cody looked at each other in apprehension as they watched a Japanese housewife reach into a pile of wiggling shrimp and carefully choose her freshly caught supper, as she placed them into her bag to take home.

"Look, Cody! Look at that over there! It looks like octopus. Look at the funny tentacles!" Bilbo squealed excitedly.

"Wow, your rabbit is certainly excited," Jimmy commented to Toshi.

"I think that they like seeing all of this," Toshi explained. "It is very different from their life on the farm in America."

"Then they should certainly like the arcade!" Jimmy chuckled.

They followed Aiko who seemed to know exactly where she was going. As Toshi and Jimmy tried to keep up with the girls, Bilbo and Cody watched in amazement as they dodged delivery trucks coming from both directions on the narrow street. The street was filled with shoppers who arrived by foot and by way of the subway. They watched as the boys' dodged pedestrian traffic, this way and that, just like watching the Pac-man game they had seen Toshi and Natsumi playing in the living room.

"I love Tokyo!" Cody declared. In all my travels to different places in America, it is the most exciting place I have visited in my life!"

"I love Tokyo too!" Bilbo agreed. "It's like it has a secret life of its very own. Look there, see that shop?"

Cody looked to see where Bilbo was looking, and off to their right he could see a very mysterious shop selling herbs, incense, and ancient cures to the ordinary pedestrian.

"I'd like very much to visit there, Toshi," Sensei said.

Toshi heard Sensei and paused for a moment. "I'd like to stop and look here," Toshi beckoned to the others.

"That would be a good plan. The store that I am going to is just up the street there, heading back to the main street," Aiko explained. "We'll probably be there for a few minutes and you'll certainly not be interested in the perfumes and jewelry that they have," Aiko commented.

"Join us there when you have finished browsing," Natsumi chattered, as they walked away.

Toshi turned off the path and walked into the shop. The two boys looked about the store in awe of its contents. One display case had numerous assorted vials containing essential oils such as dragon's blood and frankincense. Another display case had vials containing dry ingredients, such as herbs, dragon's bone, and bat wings. Still another had ancient Japanese woodblock prints by local artists. The back of the store also had antique collector's items for sale, or at least they seemed to be antique, like artful scrolls, old samurai helmets and swords, and small Buddha-styled idol images. Toshi was looking at a pair of Komainu foxes, guardians for shrine entrances.

"I don't know why, but I really want these for some reason. Maybe they could guard the rabbits?" Toshi said to Jimmy out loud.

"Can I help you?" could be heard, as an elderly Japanese gentleman approached.

Toshi looked up into the face of the man. He reminded him of his grandfather. He had a long gray beard, bald head, and his face was as wrinkled as a dried up prune. His eyes were kind and wise, and they wrinkled even more as he smiled.

"This could guard your prized possessions, yes it could," the elderly gentleman said softly, as he nodded at Toshi with a friendly twinkle in his eyes. It seemed as if he knew that Toshi was in need of the Komainu. "For you, only one thousand yen."

"You're kidding? I'll take them!" Toshi exclaimed. He watched as the old man took them gently off the shelf and brought them to the counter to be wrapped ever so carefully before being put into a special bag.

"Now you take care of these. You should guard them as well as they guard you," the elderly man instructed. "Now, if you should need anything else, I have put my business card in the bag, and remember, my name is Komatsu," he said, as he smiled and bowed.

"Yes, I will be certain to come back if ever I need anything," Toshi said, as he bowed even lower.

As Toshi and Jimmy left, incense wafted about them and followed them as they exited the shop. They walked quickly to where Natsumi stood outside a shop watching as Aiko's necklace for her mom was being wrapped in a pretty red box and placed in a decorative shopping bag of its own.

"There, we're ready to go," Natsumi said, as the four continued on their way.

They arrived outside the arcade where Bilbo and Cody could see row upon row of electrical games.

Jimmy ran in and put some coins into his favorite game. "Look! I'm a Taiko drummer! I want my pinball machine balls to hit small drums inside, as they bounce around in my game. I will have to make many small drums for them to bounce off of."

"That's a good idea, Jimmy," Toshi shouted, as he himself began to play a sumo wrestler game. "I'm going to have spinning wheels with evil creatures on them, all wrapped around like a Japanese star and when the ball hits them, they will spin. Each time they spin, they try to nip Bilbo bunny's tail, which will be just out of their reach and Bilbo will escape. Each time he escapes, the bell will ring!"

"That's really cool!" Aiko praised. "I like music, so I'm going to have the balls hit musical chimes that can form a simple melody as they fall down. If they form the right melody, all the bells will go off! I think I would like a rabbit to be holding each one of the instruments."

"That's a fantastic idea, Aiko!" Natsumi cheered, as she played her game. "I would like my pinballs to be clear like dragon jewels. If they hit the center circle, I want to make something out of cardboard or plastic that could pop open. On the outside will be a picture showing creatures chasing after the rabbit and the jewels into a bamboo forest. If the ball hits the right pin, I want the cardboard picture to pop open and show a picture inside. That picture will show the evil creatures turned to good and holding hands with the rabbit. So I will have to work on making something that will pop open. Also, I would like the balls that don't hit the middle circle to go inside holes within the pictures of each dragon where they will simply disappear and go back into the game."

"That sounds really cool! So you can use some of the pictures you've already drawn. You'll just have to make the dragons much smaller," Aiko thought out loud. "Hey, why don't you all join me at the karaoke booth so we can all sing Bilbo and Cody a song from their home?"

"All right. That would be good before we have to go home," Toshi agreed. They all proceeded to a small booth with a camera in it. Aiko picked out the song, Home on the Range, and they all began to sing.

"Home, home on the range!"

"Sounds more like Home, Home on the Wange," Cody commented, pleased by the singing. Aiko pressed the picture button and a minute later, a picture slowly came out of the machine.

"Now we have a memento of our time together. Isn't that nice?" Aiko chattered.

Bilbo and Cody watched the amazing room full of games and merry inhabitants as the four slowly exited the arcade. Soon the ringing and buzzing was far behind them as they made their way back home.

"Now we'll work on our projects until we win best display at the science fair," Jimmy chirped happily.

They soon arrived home and indeed, they did work until late, drawing their artwork together, upstairs in the attic. Toshi was able to construct his Taiko drums to make a thumping noise when the balls hit them.

With Toshi's help, Aiko was able to engineer different tones from the pieces of xylophone she had brought. She then proceeded to place them in the correct order to form a melody.

Toshi found it easy to place a piece of plastic (on which he had drawn evil creatures) on the pinball board and was able to make it loose enough to spin when the ball hit it. So he proceeded to draw several other rabbit pictures whose tails were just out of distance of the mouths of the spinning creatures that he would nail onto the board. Natsumi found her project a bit more difficult. She found that she needed to use a semi-sturdy piece of plastic that could spin and turn over when the balls hit it to show the other picture. She got the idea from a game she had and removed the plastic pieces from it. Once she discovered how to do it, she also added a few more that would reveal fortunes once they were hit.

The children worked until it was time for supper and then returned to complete their projects.

"I think everyone will be impressed at the science fair!" Toshi said when they had finished and were comparing each other's work. "Let's all make a promise to remain good friends, whoever should win."

"I like that idea!" Jimmy agreed.

"I've got it. Everyone join hands," Aiko instructed, as they formed a circle. "Now, repeat after me...

Friends we be, through thick and thin,
For if one succeeds then we all will win.
And if ever one of us needs aid,
The rest of us will form a crusade.
For this is what we pledge to sing,
No matter what the future should bring.

"That's really nice, Aiko," Natsumi commented in the now dimly lit room. "I think it is time for us to go downstairs to bed though."

"Wait, I want to put my Komainu out tonight in order for them to guard the rabbits," Toshi said, as he got his bag from the market and carefully unwrapped the figurines. "There!" he said, placing them on either side of the rabbit's cages.

The fox figurines did look very protective next to the rabbit's cages in the moonlit room as they turned off the lights for the night.

"Goodnight, bunnies," the four called out, as they exited to the stairway.

"Goodnight, good friends," the rabbits thumped back to them.

As it turned out, the four projects did very well that week at the science fair. Natsumi's project won an outstanding award for its innovativeness, and the others won honorable mentions.

Kamakura and the Dragon's Bone

~~~~~~

Chapter 9

Toshi and Natsumi were so consumed with the science fair that the time seemed to fly by for their trip to Kamakura on Saturday. They prepared by packing a little dragon dust and a little bit of everything else, just in case they should need it, and of course, they prepared the rabbits for the trip, explaining to their mom that the rabbits would enjoy the country and that Grandmother would enjoy seeing the rabbits. All was in readiness for the great trip to Kamakura.

Entering the gateway to Hokokuji, they proceeded down the well-paved path. Peeking his head out of Toshi's book bag, Bilbo could see the statue image of a mystical god-like woman, somewhat similar to others he had seen in Tokyo. As they continued down the path, they could hear a magical whispering wind sound. Cody peeked out from under the partly unzipped backpack he was in and could see the beautifully landscaped path that lay ahead of them. They passed more statues and then as they heard babbling water, they could see the source of the magical whispering sound. Bamboo started to appear and the leaves above were making the mystical noise. It was as if there was no wind, but there was.

"Is that the babbling brook already?" Toshi asked.

"No, I think I know where it is. It is almost before the temple buildings," Natsumi replied.

As they continued on, Bilbo and Cody watched as Natsumi and Toshi paid their respects to a statue that contained many images within it. They noticed at the top of it were two dragon figures protecting a temple image. Then they passed a temple bell and entered a clearing within which were many buildings.

"Come, Natsumi, we have no time to visit the temple," Toshi ordered.

They watched as Toshi and Natsumi clamored up some stepping stones and passed more small statues and into a huge bamboo forest.

"Grandfather and I liked to go here a lot," Natsumi said, as they picked their way through the bamboo. "Tea, Toshi?"

"Okay, but we can't stay long."

Again they heard the trickling of water coming from down the hillside next to where Natsumi and Toshi entered a pavilion. Natsumi ordered two teas. They watched while the Japanese women swished the green tea inside small bowls and then handed them to Toshi and Natsumi. They sat for a while under the awning of the pavilion and watched the bamboo leaves fall amidst the trickling of the water.

"Ah, much better, let's get going," Toshi instructed.

They proceeded on down the path again passing more little statues until the path became smooth.

When they began to hear the trickle of water again, Natsumi stopped. "There! See what I mean?" Natsumi said, as she looked toward three cave-like structures. "This seems just like in the riddle. Where your friends might hear the babbling brook, it's where in the end; all was took. There you must find the dragon bone, to find the gem which was lost but now is found.

"Don't you think this is where we should look?" Natsumi asked.

"Yes, by the old graves in the incinerator vault. That would be the best place to find dragon bone ash too! We'll have to be careful that no one sees us," Toshi said, as he looked over his shoulder to see if anyone was around. "Let's hurry and check the one on the left first," Toshi instructed, as he broke through the brush and ran quickly out of sight into the first cave-like opening.

Natsumi ran inside the first Yagura Cave, crouching next to Toshi as they looked inside. In the dark, they could make out small lantern -type structures from the direction in which they had entered. Deeper, in the dark abscesses of the cave, they could see large bricks on top of which were more Buddha-like images.

"Do you feel any instincts about where to look?" Toshi asked.

"No. Maybe if we brought out the key, it may lead us where to go," Natsumi answered. "Bilbo, try sticking the key outside of the book bag."

Bilbo popped his head completely out of the zipper opening and with that the key that was secured around his neck glistened in the darkness of the cave. It glistened and then emitted a light of its own which seemed to lead out of the cave. They followed it out of the cave, first looking to see if anyone was outside. Quickly, they followed as it led them past the middle cave and to the third cave. They scrambled up past the bushes and trees in order to get into the third more obscure cave. From outside, there seemed to be nothing, but as they began to follow the path of light that emitted from the magic key, they could see small lanterns like in the other caves. The cave went deeper and deeper inside unlike the other two caves. Natsumi and Toshi walked carefully as they stepped around large bricks with small statues on top like in the other caves; but the light led them on. They then reached what seemed to be the end of the cave where they could see a larger Buddha-like statue sitting upon two stones. The beam of light shone behind the large statue and they followed it. The light shone above the wall ledge behind the statue.

"Let Bilbo out so he can try touching the key at the end of the light," Natsumi instructed.

Toshi slowly removed his backpack and opened it wide on the floor of the cave. Bilbo hopped onto the old ashen-caked floor. Toshi lifted him up onto the ledge and watched as Bilbo took the key in his mouth. Bilbo tapped the key where the light shone and as he did, he had to scramble aside as a small door in the stone ledge slowly began to open.

"Wow! Look at that!" Toshi exclaimed. Toshi looked inside. He could see that the opening went deep inside without an apparent end. The light seemed to glow down inside, somewhere deeper. The opening seemed just big enough for a rabbit to enter. "The rabbits will have to go on alone I'm afraid."

"Oh, do be careful, Bilbo!" Natsumi warned.

"Can I get out, too?" Cody's muffled voice called out from inside Natsumi's bag.

"Of course, Cody, you might need to help Bilbo," Natsumi replied, as she removed her book bag and let Cody out.

"Ready, Cody?" Bilbo asked, as Natsumi placed Cody up on the ledge next to him.

"I'm as ready as you are," Cody said, as he looked deep into the small passageway.

They then hopped slowly down the semi-lit path, following it through a small ancient looking tunnel.

"Look, Bilbo, see the markings on the wall? It's just like the first tunnel markings back in Ueno Park. It has the same tanuki, crows, and those other evil creatures. Look! There's a fox too! And an evil looking dragon. Oh my, there are two rabbits! They look just like us! Look, they're being chased by all the evil creatures."

"But look here," Bilbo said who had hopped ahead. "Look at this!"

Cody hopped over to where Bilbo was standing, which he realized now was the end of the tunnel. The two were dumbfounded to find an even larger cavern at the end of the small and poorly lit tunnel. They could see a giant statue portraying a waterfall-like explosion of water and the evil creatures flying up on the stone torrents of water. Overhead flew many dragon figures swirling in the sky, and at the highest peak of stone carved water, sat a giant pearl, a real pearl that emitted a translucent glow of light.

They slowly began to realize that the tunnel floor was becoming brighter. Looking around, they realized that the tunnel was white with what could only be small crushed pieces of bone. The key around Bilbo's neck began to tremble and seemed to direct itself to a hole in the base of the stone statue. Bilbo helped fit the key into the hole and watched as once again stone seemed to move magically without anyone's help. A small drawer appeared and the two rabbits looked inside. There sat a scroll just like the others they had found before, and another small satchel. Bilbo began to reach into the drawer with his mouth when all of a sudden the earth began to shake, just like the first day they had arrived in Japan. The two rabbits braced themselves in fear, looking about the cave.

"What if the tunnel collapses?" Cody said, worried.

"Have faith!" Bilbo's voice said not too assuredly.

Then something fell to the floor, and something else. There on the tunnel floor shone the gigantic pearl. Next to it, sat a miniature dragon-like creature made out of stone that had fallen off the top of the statue.

"I guess that's the gem mentioned in the last scroll," Cody commented.

The earth stopped trembling and Bilbo retrieved the scroll.

"Cody, take the satchel and put the pearl and the dragon thing inside it," Bilbo instructed. "I have enough of my own to carry."

Cody tried his best to slip the satchel open and then pushed and pushed the pearl about the floor.

"Cody, are you having trouble?" Bilbo asked, as he watched Cody go in circles around the statue, as the pearl kept rolling out of his reach.

"Ah, just give me a little time and I'll get it." Finally, he got it into the satchel, then the small dragon figurine.

"Oh yes, we can't forget. We're supposed to gather dragon bone. Do you suppose that's why the bones shine in here?" Bilbo thought out loud.

"That must be it. I'll gather as much as I can in this satchel." Bilbo helped push up bone fragments and ash in a pile and they both pushed it into the satchel, a little at a time. They had just got the ties secured when the earth began to tremble again, this time with much more power.

The cave wall began to crumble down upon them.

"Let's get out of here!" Bilbo squealed.

"I'm with you!" agreed Cody, as the two rabbits headed down the tunnel as fast as their legs could carry them.

Outside, Toshi and Natsumi waited for the rabbits. The main cave they were in also began to crumble apart and they crouched near the rabbit's tunnel, watching and waiting.

"Hurry, Bilbo and Cody!" Natsumi shouted into the small tunnel entrance. They could hear rumbling and the crunching of rock and stone coming from where Bilbo and Cody had disappeared. Toshi and Natsumi looked desperately at one another, unable to do anything but wait, as they heard a gigantic rumble from inside and then watched as a huge pile of dust spurt out from the small tunnel. And then all was quiet.

Inside the tunnel, Bilbo and Cody tried desperately to make their way through the never-ending tunnel, as stones and cave fell away behind them. Then all went dark as they were buried in the debris; still the earth trembled. In the dark, Bilbo had hit his head against the rock wall that had fallen into his exit way. Cody had ran into Bilbo and they both sat in a very small opening. The air seemed stuffy and it was very dark except for a small light emanating from within the satchel that Cody was carrying tied around his neck.

"We're trapped," Bilbo said, dazed.

"Bilbo, doesn't this remind you of something?" Cody asked.

"Yeah, it's just like when you helped me out of the barrel a long time ago on the farm, back in America."

"I think maybe we'll make it out again," Cody muttered, as he pawed the tunnel debris where the exit used to be. "It seems like tunnels are forever a rabbit's business, doesn't it?"

"I'm very quickly getting tired of tunnels," Bilbo complained. "Remember my son, Binky's, experience? I tell you, I'll be happy if we never see another tunnel again."

"Cody, open the satchel and take out the dragon," Sensei instructed from out of the darkness.

"Gee, I forgot you were here with us," Cody replied, as he began to gnaw on the satchel ties. Finally, opening the bag, he grabbed the dragon figurine out.

"Now, if you place the pearl next to it while you sprinkle a little of the bone dust onto the dragon, I think it may help us," Sensei instructed.

"All right," Cody murmured. Cody followed Sensei's instructions, sat down, and watched while nothing seemed to happen. Then the light from the pearl seemed to grow brighter. The eyes in the dragon seemed to flicker in the dark. Then ever so slowly, like a crocodile coming out of hibernation, it seemed to be coming to life, its eyes fixed ever so lustfully upon the pearl. The three of them watched in amazement as the dragon eerily came to life, grabbed the ever-so-much-larger pearl with both claws, and stowed it under itself.

"It looks like a mother holding its egg!" Bilbo shouted. "What if it flies away with it and leaves us in here?"

"Don't worry, where it makes a way out, we will follow, but you must quickly grab onto its tail," Sensei ordered.

Bilbo quickly followed Sensei's instructions and grabbed onto its tail. Cody gathered up his satchel and grabbed onto Bilbo's tail. They watched as the little dragon snarled and sniffed, looking about the collapsed tunnel wall. As the dragon sniffed, it became more interested in the direction of the exit. Then it began to gather up its breath and with a big roaring noise, it blasted a burst of fire and gas that exploded the stone and rock in front of them just enough to bust some of it loose. Soon they could see the opening of the tunnel wall again ahead of them.

"Hold on tight you two. He's going to make a break for it!" Sensei shouted.

Bilbo and Cody held on tight as the dragon began to magically surge through the air just like the jet Bilbo and Cody had flown to Japan on. Out of the tunnel, it surged on its small magical wings that glistened now with dragon dust. Bilbo and Cody hung on tight for dear life.

"Natsumi! Toshi! Help! We're holding onto the tail of the dragon! Hold your hands over the tunnel. Grab the dragon and take the pearl from the dragon when it comes out of the tunnel!" Sensei shouted.

Outside the tunnel where Natsumi and Toshi had been waiting, they looked in disbelief at one another, but without question, held their hands over the tunnel exit and waited until something hit their hands hard with a thump. When they saw parts of a round pearl-like object, they tried to grab it loose.

"Ow, something feels scratchy!" Natsumi complained, wincing, as she struggled to keep the round pearl in her grasp.

"Ow, you're right," Toshi grunted, as he also struggled to get a grip. "Got it!"

Toshi fell back as the pearl broke loose. Then looking to see what had been holding the pearl, he could see what appeared to be a miniature dragon statue with a glint of light in its eyes that seemed to be almost lifelike. It wiggled slightly and then sat still. Holding onto the tail of the dragon, they could see Bilbo.

"Is Cody there?" Natsumi asked.

"Yes!" a voice called out from behind Bilbo.

"We were afraid for you guys," Natsumi said, as she picked the dragon figurine out of the tunnel's way. A dusty Bilbo stepped out of the tunnel and onto the ledge, and out followed Cody.

"What happened in there?" Toshi asked.

"We'll tell you all about it later, but could we read the scroll now? I'm curious to find out what will happen next," Cody explained, as he opened the satchel and pulled out the scroll with his teeth. "Here, you can help open it and read it," he said to Natsumi. "You were the one who knew where to look."

Leaning on the stone ledge, Natsumi opened the miniature scroll and began to read...

> *Soldiers of peace will join and rise,*
> *When once you mix the handful of supplies.*
> *But first and for the second time,*
> *you must retrieve the gem you once did find,*
> *which once was lost, but now was found.*
> *Where you once met in the distant past,*
> *the white dragon that has gone astray,*
> *to join the others on the appointed day.*
> *It is this one who leads the others,*
> *that you must befriend,*
> *To purge all evil, and bring peace without end.*

"What does that mean? I don't know of any white dragon. And I never found a gem before that I lost. What could it mean?" Natsumi thought out loud.

"I don't know of any such white dragon," Sensei agreed glumly.

"Nor I," Toshi commented.

Toshi and Natsumi sat down on the stone blocks while Cody and Bilbo sat upon the stone ledge thinking long and hard.

"Wait a minute! Back in America, I had to retrieve a magic prism from a white woodhog called Windwalker. Could the white woodhog represent the dragon?" Bilbo asked excitedly.

"You must be right," Sensei agreed, his head and arms poking up out of Bilbo's fur.

"Oh my!" Natsumi shouted. "Look at Sensei. He's grown red scales across the top of his back. Sensei, you look like a small dragon, you even have little legs now."

"It has begun. The beginning of the end of evil. We must hurry before evil is on our tails."

"But how do we get to America to get the magic prism jewel?" Cody asked, puzzled.

"You saw it. The pearl, the magical giver of life," Sensei replied. "If I take it in my arms, you can hold onto my tail and I can fly on the wings of the magical pearl, but we must be careful because all that is evil will be upon us trying to get the pearl."

"But what about our parents? How will we be able to go?" Toshi asked.

"I promise that with the time difference between the east and the west, your parents will never know you were gone...unless something happens to you," Sensei answered solemnly.

"When do we go?" Toshi asked valiantly.

"It is imperative that we go immediately," Sensei replied, as he slipped down Bilbo's fur to the floor of the stone ledge. "Toshi, could you go gather some water from the brook with one of the cups on the altar there? I'll need it to drink down the herb mixture," Sensei ordered Toshi. "I'm sure the powers that be would approve. Now, Natsumi, you get the ingredients out of Cody's satchel."

In the dimly lit cave, Natsumi removed the dragon bone ash and the last herb that had been left in the bag for them inside the Kamakura tunnel.

"Now, place some of the herb and dragon bone ash into the remaining cup on the altar, over there," he said, pointing, "then stir it up," Sensei continued. "Ah, now, Toshi...pour the water into the other cup while Natsumi stirs."

Toshi and Natsumi did as Sensei told them.

"Now, place the cup in front of me and tip it so that I may drink it," Sensei continued. Natsumi tipped the cup in front of Sensei and he began to drink. Pausing for a moment, he crawled over to the carved dragon statue and gnawed on it, then continued to drink. This he did on and off until the cup was empty. The four of them watched and wondered what the mixture was supposed to do. They began to notice a cloud surround Sensei, as he seemed to grow larger. His skin grew thinner and thinner

71

as it stretched larger and larger. Within a minute, he had already grown too large for the ledge, and they watched while he pounced down to the cave floor. Outside the cave, they could hear thunder and lightning crashing, where a few minutes ago, it had been sunny. They could see gigantic clouds billowing and exploding in the sky, which just a few minutes before had been totally clear. Then their eyes turned back in disbelief to see Sensei as translucent scales sprouted from every portion of his once smooth silkworm body. Growing larger and larger until his head protruded from the cave's entrance, Sensei continued to go under metamorphosis until finally he had no choice but to exit the cave.

Sensei ordered one last instruction. "Hurry, gather your satchels and climb upon my back, all of you, there is no time to waste. The evil ones have sensed the presence of the magic pearl."

Natsumi and Toshi gathered Bilbo, Cody, and the other objects they had found in their backpacks, and without question, climbed upon Sensei's back. Sensei turned, grabbed a hold of the magic pearl in the dark, and then strained his neck at the cave exit, looking first from one side to the other. Outside, the clouds continued to divide and explode. From out of every corner of the forest (that had now turned dark) he could see tanuki, oni, and many other creatures that were usually of a peaceful temperament, growling and snarling and approaching ever faster.

"Hold tight," Sensei shouted, as he gathered a huge breath of air, then spread his large, green, translucent wings and began to flap them. They watched as Sensei turned back around and snatched the remainder of the dragon statue in his gigantic, tooth-riddled mouth. They could hear it crunch as he gnawed it to shreds and then swallowed it down. He then breathed deeply as he flapped his wings and rose in the air. As they took off, Natsumi and the others looked down and could see the earth getting farther and farther away. There at the cave exit, they could see an assortment of evil looking characters, snarling in rage at them as they rose above the bamboo forest and ever higher into the sky, which was rumbling and cracking with lightning. The rain and the angry clouds pelted them with hail as they rose ever higher, until they were finally clear of them. Then their speed seemed to increase as they watched the clouds disappear behind them, incredibly faster and faster. They watched as they passed jets that were on their way from Narita airport, heading west. On Sensei flew, at an incredible speed, with Natsumi and Toshi burrowing themselves under his soft scales to protect themselves from the elements.

"Hold on tight you guys," Bilbo shouted out to Toshi, as he and Cody peeked out from their book bags at the vast expanse of open sky.

A Trip In Time

~~~~~~~~~~~~~~~~~~~~

Chapter 10

On and on they flew, but not nearly as long as their trip to Japan. Day turned to night and finally they could feel Sensei decelerating. They could smell the sweet familiar scent of alfalfa nearby in the darkness.

"Look, Bilbo, that looks like the silo where we met Windwalker last year!" Cody shouted, as he looked down. They watched, as the silo grew closer and then as Sensei landed on it. The moon shone down on the silo and made it light enough to see their old hopping grounds.

"Wow, that was awesome!" Toshi exclaimed.

"I'm glad you liked the ride, Toshi," Sensei replied in a raspy dragon-like voice. Turning his long scaly neck toward them, he asked, "But where to now?"

"I think over to the white building there in the corner of the pine trees," Bilbo replied. "But first, why don't you fly overhead there to the left, and we'll let the donkeys know we're here. We may need their help, too."

"All right," Sensei agreed, as he swooped off the silo and circled around the donkeys' pasture.

"Guido, Sugar, Daisy, Delilah...it's us...are you up?" Bilbo and Cody called from overhead.

They watched and waited for their old donkey friends to emerge from the barn in the clearing.

"Hey, remember us?" Bilbo called out from above.

The donkeys were startled by the image in the sky that glowed peculiarly in the night sky. They backed away from the swirling image.

"Wait, it's Natsumi...and Bilbo and Cody...you know us!" Natsumi shouted.

Guido stopped and squinted in the dark until he recognized Natsumi. Then Sensei landed on the ground in front of them.

Natsumi and Toshi let go of Sensei's scales and slid to the ground.

"We're here to get the prism jewel back from the woodhogs. Do you know anything about where they might be keeping it?" Bilbo asked, as he popped his head from the back of Toshi's bag.

"I'm sure they keep it down by the river in that fortress where they held Binky and Chuckles hostage before," Guido replied.

"We could find Windwalker," Daisy suggested. "He'll know where it is."

"Why don't you find him and tell him to meet us at the rabbit barn," Bilbo asked. "We'll be talking to Binky and the others there."

"Will you be going down there right away?" Delilah asked.

"Yes, please hurry!" Sensei instructed.

The donkeys were quite willing to leave the strange company of the large dragon and were soon on their way to find Windwalker.

Sensei, Natsumi, and Toshi walked across the farmyard to the rabbits' barn. They could see Bilbo and Cody's old owners inside the large picture window watching television.

"Shhh," Natsumi whispered to Sensei, as he tried to walk as quietly as a dragon could, his tail held up high, so as not to cause a dragging sound on the gravel driveway that they crossed. Reaching the rabbit barn, Natsumi and Toshi removed Bilbo and Cody from their book bags and waited for the two rabbits to announce themselves inside the barn.

Bilbo and Cody hopped through the open doorway into their old surroundings. Above, the familiar rabbit cages hung from the ceiling.

"Gee, I kind of miss my old home," Bilbo commented.

"But our new home is good, too, don't you think?" Cody responded.

"Who's there?" a voice called out of the darkness, and all of a sudden, there was the sound of many rabbits thumping their back legs hard on their cages, threateningly.

"It's us, Bilbo and Cody," Bilbo answered.

"No, they're in Japan. Step closer so we can see you," a rabbit answered in the darkness.

Bilbo and Cody hopped closer to the voice in the dark.

"Oh, it's you, Father!" Binky exclaimed, as he recognized Bilbo in the moonlight.

"It's Bilbo and Cody! They're back!" one rabbit shouted after another. "They've come back from Japan!"

"Welcome back!" they heard their old friends calling.

"Father! What are you doing here?" Binky cried.

"We've come to get the prism back from the woodhogs!"

"And we've brought a Japanese dragon to help us!" Cody shouted. "A real dragon! We rode here all the way from Japan on it."

"No, I don't believe it!" Binky exclaimed.

"Come out and see for yourself!" Sensei's raspy dragon voice called from outside.

"Wait, you must see your grandchildren," Binky said. "See here," he said, motioning to the cage next to him. "Sarah is now living in the rabbit barn with me. You have three grandchildren now," he said, as the rabbit in the nest box next to Binky waved her paw.

"Chuckles and Buster moved out of state to new rabbitries and they're doing well." Binky unlatched his cage in his usual manner and soon was hopping out the door with Bilbo, their shadows joined together.

Outside, Sensei waited, his dragon shape looming overhead under the magic of the full moon.

"We don't have long to visit," he warned.

"No, we don't," another unexpected voice said out of the darkness.

A glow of light appeared around the image of someone whom the rabbits hadn't seen in a long time. There before their eyes, stood their former elder, Snowflake, who had long since passed away.

"Time is running out!" Snowflake informed them, his fluffy white angora fur glowing in the moonlight. "The woodhogs have been committing all sorts of atrocities. They have been plotting with creatures from other countries and have planted the seeds of war among them."

"But how could they? They're just not that smart," Bilbo objected.

"By causing misinterpretations, miscommunications, and mistrust between nations of people," Snowflake answered.

"And just how does an animal do that?" Toshi asked.

"By worshipping the prism jewel as if it were a god. They think they will have more power once the world is in chaos," Snowflake's figure explained in the darkness.

"And not only that, they now intend to give the prism over to a much more evil creature from the east this very night!" Snowflake exclaimed.

They were interrupted by the sudden appearance of the four donkeys, the pony, and a white fluffy creature that sat upon Guido's back.

"Windwalker, they found you!" Bilbo cried out.

"Yes, I've come just as it has been foretold," the white figure responded.

"What do you mean?" Bilbo asked.

"Just as it was written on the scroll that I found when I found the prism by the river," Windwalker replied. "The scroll said:

When the time comes, and all the world depends,
Gather this and all your friends.
To take this gem, and the other four,
To the rising waters, where once was more.
Cast away these jewels, and all evil will be devoured,
To cleanse the world of all false desires.

Then gather your friends, of a like fold,
Who have been waiting, as times foretold.
To gather the magical waters, to be unfurled,
To spread peace across the world.

"I think it has something to do with why I can fly," Windwalker concluded.

"I know exactly what it means now," Bilbo answered. "It means that you and Sensei and whatever other dragons we can find are supposed to gather the jewels and the powders we have been provided. Then we are to meet at the appropriate time at the fountain in Ueno Park. Then, when all evil is following the jewels, cast them into the water where all the evil creatures will follow, since they want the jewels."

"Then what? The evil creatures will have the jewels. Then what will we do?" Cody questioned.

"It doesn't matter," Sensei responded. "Once they have the jewels, they and all the jewels will be sucked down into the fountain. Then we spread peace and understanding by bringing the cleansing water to all places on earth."

"What did you say? Did you say I was a dragon?" Windwalker asked.

"I believe as soon as you eat the elixir, like I mixed for myself, you will also become a dragon, maybe just not as big, since I had more dragon ash to consume," Sensei answered.

"Natsumi, could you find us some water and gather the ingredients from the Kamakura satchel, like I asked for last time?" Sensei asked.

"There usually is a jug or two of water in the rabbit barn. I'll go find some," Natsumi offered.

While Natsumi gathered the concoction, the others watched for trouble. "Maybe we better go inside; they might see us from the house, especially Sensei and the pony," Cody warned. "Our old keeper is always watching to make sure the horse and donkeys aren't loose."

"Good idea," Sensei agreed, as he slowly dragged his huge dragon body into the large pole barn.

The others followed and formed a circle inside with the rabbit cages surrounding them in a U-shape.

"Quite a sight we make! Four donkeys, a dragon, Snowflake, Windwalker, Trigger the pony, and all these rabbits," Toshi commented. "We're living a dream. We have a fictional dragon, the spirit of a deceased rabbit elder, and now a strange white woodhog who is really a dragon also?"

"I've found it," Natsumi chattered enthusiastically, as she brought the water to the middle of the barn where the group had gathered. Placing a rabbit dish on the dirt floor, she poured the water, herb, and ash from the Kamakura satchel into it and stirred it with her finger.

"There! Drink that!" Natsumi offered, nodding at Windwalker as she stepped back.

The furry white-winged woodhog stepped forward out of the circle, looked about at the others who waited for him, and then proceeded to drink from the rabbit dish until it was empty. Nothing seemed to happen right away. They watched breathlessly for something to happen and then all at once, Windwalker began to glow with a white light. Then he began to grow and grow and grow. No scales, just growing quite large and elongated throughout his head, body, and wings. Like Sensei, the larger he grew, the more translucent he became, glowing and glistening with light within. His chest and abdomen grew wider to provide dragon lung air lift capability, and his neck grew considerably longer, befitting a dragon. Finally, the transformation seemed to be complete. His white fluffy hair glistened in the night.

Windwalker stretched his wings out over the tops of the rabbit cages that hung from the ceiling. "I believe I am ready," he said.

"But we need a plan," Sensei replied. "Do you know where they keep the prism?"

"Down by the river, in their cement fortress, but they will be bringing it out tonight," Windwalker advised. "Boar-acc will be leading others. That is how evil he has become with the prism. I didn't think that the prism would work at all for the powers of evil, or that they were smart enough to use it, but apparently, there is evil as well as good in it, just as within us all."

"Then this is what we must do," Sensei instructed. "We'll need to entice him with the dragon dust in a path leading to the magic pearl and then all of you will have to jump him in order to get the prism. I know it sounds hard, but all depends upon it."

"But what if he gets the pearl?" Bilbo asked. "That could mean disaster."

"Don't worry, I will keep it in my claws, camouflaged under the dirt and leaves," Sensei answered. "I suggest that the donkeys and the pony keep the other woodhogs and creatures away with their hooves, and that Windwalker and I be the main ones waiting to grab the prism from Boar-acc, since we have the most strength, the ability to fly if need be, and the claws, the better to grab it. Natsumi and Toshi can also be on hand in case it is dropped. They can be the ones to spread the dragon dust. We'll have to be quiet on our way, so that we're not discovered," he said, as he looked at the circle of friends that surrounded him. "Once we get a hold of the prism, I'm afraid we may need to make a hasty departure, not just away from the river, but directly to Japan...and Windwalker, you must come with us...so be prepared. Are you all ready?"

"Ready!" Windwalker agreed.

"We're ready!" the four donkeys and the pony shouted in unison.

"Ready!" Bilbo and Cody shouted.

"Ready!" Binky shouted.

"You're coming, Binky?" Bilbo asked.

"I wouldn't want to miss an adventure with my father," Binky said, winking at Bilbo.

"I will go ahead and scout our way," Snowflake, the elder spirit offered, as he glided out of the barn and waited for the others to follow. Snowflake looked up toward the moon, and as if he commanded it, clouds appeared from nowhere and covered the moon, blocking its light and providing cover.

One by one, they left the safety of the rabbit barn and entered the dangerous night. Snowflake provided a small trickle of light the size of a firefly for them to follow as they made their way around the yard to the open gate that led across the railroad tracks, across the open alfalfa field, through the forest and down to the river. Ever so slowly, stealthily, they crept their way, quietly across the alfalfa field. Then they inched their way toward the woodhogs' rock fortress until they saw some activity down by the river.

The woodhogs were holding some kind of ceremony. Amidst the woodhogs were several other creatures of unknown origin, creatures with huge teeth and claws. Drums, woodhog drums, beat a repetitive thump-thump, thump-thump-thump, over and over again. They could see Boar-acc with the prism strung around his neck sitting on a rock in the center of it all.

"How are we to get Boar-acc to leave the others?" Bilbo whispered to Sensei.

"I will hide myself behind the rocks and hold my arm out with the pearl in it. Toshi will spread the dragon dust from there back to as far as he can toward Boar-acc to lead him here. Then when we're ready, the donkeys and the pony will start kicking up a ruckus and spreading out the group. Binky, Bilbo, and Cody can try to lure Boar-acc this way until he catches sight of

81

the dragon dust that will then entice him to the pearl. Are you ready, Toshi?"

"Ready!" Toshi answered. Then with his satchel open, he stepped softly and began sprinkling dragon dust as he slipped from tree to tree, until he was as close as he could get to the gathering.

Sensei signaled the go-ahead to the donkeys and the pony. Then the five of them broke up the ceremony by nipping, thrashing, and kicking at the entire group. Bilbo, Cody, and Binky ran out in front of Boar-acc who instinctively snarled and immediately gave chase, following them directly to the path of the dragon dust. They watched as he sniffed suspiciously, but the lure of the bewitching dragon dust overcame him. He followed the path until he caught eye of the magic pearl...its iridescent beauty shimmering in a sudden burst of moonlight. He reached out to grab it, and at once, Sensei grabbed a firm hold of Boar-acc. Windwalker also swooped out of the sky and upon Boar-acc, grabbing at the prism about his neck.

Boar-acc snarled angrily, aware of the betrayal and desperate not to lose his coveted source of power, he clutched the prism tightly. He broke it free of Windwalker's grasp and shoved it down his throat in one big disgusting gulp.

"We'll have to take him with us to Japan!" Sensei roared. "Toshi and Natsumi, get Bilbo and Cody and get on! Hurry! Windwalker, put Binky on the pony's back and take this pearl. Let's make sure our friends make it safely home and then we've got to leave!"

Toshi and Natsumi quickly tucked Bilbo and Cody back into their bags and climbed aboard Sensei's back. Windwalker swooped down, gathered Binky, and sat him down on Trigger's back. Then he grabbed the pearl from Sensei's claw in order that Sensei could get a better hold of the slobbering woodhog. The group of woodhogs and creatures were scattered about looking for Boar-acc, but couldn't locate him. Before they really knew what was happening, Sensei had him firmly in his grip and they watched as Boar-acc emitted belching snarls and grunts and the two lifted upward into the moonlit sky. The donkeys and pony were already on their way out of the forest with Binky. Snowflake, who was overlooking the conflict, squinted upward at the moon and once again clouds passed over and provided them cover in which to slip out of the forest and across the field back home before the others could tell where they were headed. Before long, they were returning Binky to the safety of the rabbit barn.

"So long, Father! I will tell your grandchildren about our great adventure and about how we helped bring peace to the world," Binky shouted to Bilbo, as Windwalker dipped his white fluffy wing to wave goodbye. Sensei waited overhead on the other side of the pine trees with Boar-acc thrashing precariously in his claws.

"Bye now, Binky!" Bilbo shouted back. The pony and donkeys whinnied their goodbyes to Windwalker, Snowflake, Sensei, and the others, as they rose higher in the sky. They watched as Windwalker, pearl in hand, grabbed hold of Sensei's tail and they heard Bilbo and Cody calling goodbye from atop Toshi and Natsumi's backpacks as they too waved their goodbyes to their American friends below.

"Back to Japan for the final test!" Sensei called out from above, and then they were spinning back through time and space with great haste, back to where the enchantment began.

They traveled on through the darkness, and every once in a while, they could hear Boar-acc grunting and snarling along the way. All the while, the prism was trapped within his stomach.

Finally, they arrived back in the forest of Kamakura. Sensei and Windwalker eased downward until they arrived directly in front of the cave from which Sensei and the others had lifted off.

"Now Toshi and Natsumi, you go back home with your parents today," Sensei instructed. "We've arrived back at the same time we left. We'll have to meet you tonight outside your attic window. I want you to gather the other gems and bring them with you. Be wary, once they are uncovered from the protection of the water, we will have to protect you, and so you will have to climb directly onto our backs from the attic window. Do you think you can do that?"

"Yes, we can do it!" Natsumi cheered.

"And remember to bring all the ingredients you have gathered, and the dragon dust," Sensei further instructed.

"We'll be waiting and ready. As soon as it's time for bedtime, we'll meet you," Toshi agreed.

"Until then, we bid you a safe journey," Sensei said, as he hastily lifted off with Windwalker following closely. "We'll wait at Benton-do Temple until dark."

Then with a big whoosh of air they were gone and Toshi and Natsumi were left to make their own way home through the now again serene bamboo forest. The two never said a word, but seemed awfully quiet as they later bid their goodbyes to their grandmother and they and their parents made the two hour trip back to Tokyo.

Whir. Whir. The sound of the train made a lulling sound as Natsumi, Toshi, Cody, and Bilbo slept on the train on their way back to Tokyo.

"I think they missed their grandmother. It was good for them," Mrs. Hashimoto commented.

"Good for me, too," Mr. Hashimoto replied. "Lately, I have been under a lot of stress. What with all the upsets in our world peace efforts, it seems that terrorism is on the rise and we don't know how to neutralize the situation. We don't know why people just can't help improve world situations instead of trying to cause destruction."

"Well, you know, it is a much harder, stronger thing to swallow one's pride and take what may appear to be a weaker stance and abstain from force. We all have the dragon within us, but it is a much harder thing to harness the dragon and release the rabbit inside. Do you understand what I'm trying to say?" Mrs. Hashimoto asked.

"Yes, it is a much harder thing to control one's great pride and temper when others can't," Mr. Hashimoto confirmed, as he enjoyed the country view from outside the train.

"I can't tell you why, but my woman's intuition tells me that if you continue your work, you will be rewarded for your efforts," Mrs. Hashimoto consoled.

"Yes, tomorrow always holds promise if you believe in the best in your fellow man and in good overall," Mr. Hashimoto said, as he daydreamed about someday accomplishing world peace and they hastily made their way home.

Facing the Vortex of Evil
~~~~~~~~~~~~~~~~~~~~~~~~~~~~~~~~
Chapter 11

They hadn't been home for more than a half hour, when there was a knock at the Hashimoto's door.

"Who could that be on a Sunday night?" Mrs. Hashimoto asked despondently.

"I hope not work," Mr. Hashimoto replied.

"Ah, Mr. Hashimoto, you're home," the man at the door greeted. "We've been trying to contact you all day. Haven't you checked your answering machine?"

"Well no, I've been unpacking. I've just gotten home."

Toshi and Natsumi were in the TV room playing games already.

"Haven't you been watching what's happening on television?" the man asked.

"No, there is no television at my mother's house in Kamakura," he replied.

"I suggest that you turn it on," the man instructed.

Mr. Hashimoto made his way to where Toshi and Natsumi were playing. "You two must go to bed. I have business in here," he ordered.

After the two left the room, they bid their goodnights to their mother and then snuck to the heating vent in the attic to overhear their conversation. Their father turned the television to a news station where they could hear an urgent news broadcast being made.

"Right now, reporting live from on sight, the worst disaster in decades. Explosions have occurred at six different locations across the world. There is no explanation for the reasoning of the violence, but a note left at one disaster area claims responsibility and states that it is in the name of their leader, Boar-acc the horrible."

"You must come with us to report the government's responses to the disasters. Hurry, you have much to be briefed on," the man said.

"This is an ugly matter. We must go at once and try to offer assistance," Mr. Hashimoto responded, as he began walking toward the door. They could hear him in the distance as he told their mother he was going out and they heard the door close shut.

"Toshi, we need to hurry," Natsumi said, as she removed Bilbo from his cage and put him in her book bag.

"Do be careful!" Double D and Juliet cried in unison, as they kissed him goodbye.

Toshi left the room and soon returned with the three remaining pouches and the jar of dragon dust. Placing them into Natsumi's book bag, he could hear a whooshing noise outside the window.

"Is it them?" Toshi asked Natsumi.

Natsumi ran to the window and pushed it open. "Yes, they are waiting outside, we need to hurry. Sensei's got Boar-acc tied up, but he's struggling to get free."

"I'll put the jewels in my bag with Cody," Toshi said, as he quickly took Cody out and put him into his book bag. "There might be trouble."

They were soon out the window. Natsumi climbed onto Sensei's green scaly back first and pulled out a couple of the red scales to make a more comfortable seat. Then as Sensei flew off and waited, Windwalker glided into place at the window and waited while Toshi clamored onto his back. As Toshi grabbed his translucent fur, they both headed toward Ueno Park.

It was no time before they came to the Shinobazu Pond where the golden dragon swooped in front of them in a rage. Natsumi and Toshi had to cling tightly to Sensei and Windwalker, as the golden dragon continued to cause air turbulence.

"What's going on?" Toshi shouted.

"The dragon is after something," Natsumi exclaimed. "Oh no! Look! There's Father down there with that man!"

Cody strained to see, as well as Bilbo. They could see Mr. Hashimoto outside Benton-do Temple with the man from the house.

"That's no man, that's the white fox person, the one we saw before in the house," Bilbo said, his head sticking out of the bag.

"He must be leading your father into a trap," Cody fretted.

"Argh," Boar-acc slobbered from below, inside Sensei's claws. "You see, there is no winning, we are many in number!"

They watched as they flew closer and the two figures walked down the pathway lit by the ancient Chinese-styled stone lanterns. One by one, the lanterns flared up, as if forming a landing strip for the golden dragon to find its way to eat their father. The golden dragon was almost upon him as they raced to catch up. Dragon flight without jet stream was not that exacting, nor that fast. Sensei and Windwalker did the best they could to speed up, but all of a sudden, they seemed to hit the very same barrier that kept the golden dragon within. They spun around again and hit it with their chests, with all their force, but to no avail.

"Grandfather! Help us!" Natsumi cried out while at the same time reaching into her backpack for the magic pearl. Surely, she thought, the pearl, the giver of life, might help, if only to distract the dragon from her father.

Natsumi's father looked back and up, just in time to see the golden dragon swooping down upon him; it seemed to have no sense of the pearl.

Natsumi clutched the magic pearl in her hands, closed her eyes, and concentrated as hard as she could. "Grandfather, help Father!" she cried out, and as she did, great billowing clouds began to form around the Shinobazu Pond.

In the next instant, the golden dragon had Natsumi's father in its claws and carried him away, deeper into Ueno Park. The golden dragon had broken free of its barrier, the barrier that had been its prison for thousands of years. At the same instant, Sensei and Windwalker were through the barrier of clouds and followed the dragon's path, prepared for battle. They followed the golden dragon as it landed on the top corner of a five-story pagoda. It roared as it lifted its head and bellowed loudly into the night air. The fire from its breath heated the building's spiral tip to an ember red, while Mr. Hashimoto dangled in its grip off the curled edge of the pagoda roof.

"Father!" Natsumi cried out.

"Natsumi!" Mr. Hashimoto shouted back, as he looked up to see his daughter riding on the back of a green dragon.

"Grandfather! Where are you?" Natsumi screamed.

It was at this moment that the earth began to tremble and quake. Light emanated from a small helmet-shaped building, and as it did, the steeple began to shake and then lift off and fall to the ground. At the same time, the face of a great Buddha slowly lifted out of the opening in the top and rose into the sky, suspended by a great ball of light. It hovered mysteriously, as if awakening from a deep sleep. Then its eyes opened, emitting an even greater white light as it began to glide toward the grand fountain. They all watched in amazement at the fantastic occurrence, the golden dragon even dazed for the moment.

Sensei turned his neck back and ordered Natsumi to the business at hand. "Natsumi, you must concentrate and do as I say. You must wait to give up the pearl at the head of the fountain at precisely the time I say and not before. It's the only way. You must trust that Bilbo, Cody, Toshi, and Windwalker can place the gems simultaneously at all four corners of the fountain, while at the same time you and I will place the pearl at the top of the fountain water. It must be done exactly as this, or else all will be lost. Do you understand?"

"I will do as you and Grandfather have told me," Natsumi answered, as she watched the Great Buddha's face glide to a stop and hover over the top of the fountain.

"Did you others hear?" Sensei called out. "I will give the signal when to place the gems at the corners simultaneously.

Windwalker and I must let Bilbo and Cody down so they can do their job."

Natsumi could see the golden dragon flying past them with her father in its clutches. She quickly distributed the gems carefully placing the blue one in Bilbo's mouth, the green one in Cody's, and the red one she handed to Toshi.

"Toshi," Sensei instructed, "you had better hide the gem in your mouth also. It might help ward off the evil creatures that are after it."

Advice given a little too late it would seem because there were already swarms of crows and tanuki surrounding the fountain. From further away, there approached ghostly figures of fallen Samurai warriors, which in turn drew hideous oni creatures who appeared overhead.

"It's too late," Boar-acc grunted from beneath Sensei and Natsumi. "Our plan is already taking form."

"But our plan is also," Sensei objected, as he nodded at Windwalker and transferred Boar-acc from his claws to Windwalker's. Then Sensei waited overhead with Natsumi holding the precious pearl.

Bilbo and Cody, in return, headed for their designated corners, but were being pursued by the tanuki and crows that clawed to obtain the gems from their mouths. Both Cody and Bilbo felt the clamp of the tanuki's mouths on their hindquarters when they both resorted to the trick they had learned at the Yoshinobu gravesite. Natsumi watched below as she witnessed Bilbo and Cody disappear, and in their place were foxes that resembled the Komainu that Toshi had purchased earlier that week. They turned and snarled at the tanuki who looked confused and let go of their prey. The transformed rabbits took their positions at the far north corners of the fountain.

Toshi had reached his position and Windwalker settled down on the hard ground of the fourth corner, holding Boar-acc firmly in his grasp.

"Too late," Boar-acc roared. "You have done exactly what we had planned anyway."

Boar-acc suddenly began to grow in size until he, too, was the height of the fountain's water head. The golden dragon, which was preoccupied with Mr. Hashimoto, had joined Natsumi and Sensei at the head of the fountain. It seemed to be barely restraining itself from eating its prey.

Boar-acc, who had now reached the size of a full-blown Godzilla, called out, "Give me the pearl and I will command the golden dragon to let your father free."

"Concentrate, Natsumi. Do as your grandfather taught you," Sensei instructed.

"No, Boar-acc," Natsumi shouted. "It is you that must give up the prism or we will throw the jewels into the water and you and your companions will be sucked down into the fountain for eternity. You see, I know the truth, the true way to power, and the pearl only gives power for good, or did you forget that?"

"She's right, Boar-acc. You have become obsessed with your hunger for power. But the only true power does not come from doing bad deeds but from doing good deeds. As you can see, you may be big, but you have no real power," Sensei coaxed. "Even the child knows. Look, even the Great Buddha has awakened to purify and remind you of the right way. If you want true power, you must do no harm and recognize your place in the world as to serve others."

Natsumi looked to her right where she could see her father gasping in the dragon's claws, then she strained to see the Buddha that hovered over the fountain as if wondering what to do.

Then she heard Bilbo's small voice from somewhere down below call out, "Natsumi, give the pearl to Sensei to crush in the water. The water can cleanse away all that is bad. This is what I have learned from you in Japan."

"Here, Sensei," Natsumi said sadly. "You can smash the pearl." She handed it over to Sensei's upraised claw. Then reaching her arm back into her backpack, she removed the satchels of herbs and waited for Sensei to crush the pearl.

Boar-acc looked first at Windwalker below, who remained small, but the sparkling of his dragon dust in the moonlight that shone on his marvelous shimmering wings blinded him. Then he looked back at Sensei who fluttered high over the fountain head and once again, the shimmering dragon dust blinded him. It was at that instant they could hear Boar-acc's cry of anguish and a terrible gagging sound, as a foul smell penetrated the night air.

They could hear a thud and a loud splash as the fountain began to surge higher. It was at this precise moment that Natsumi saw Sensei crush the fabulous magical pearl and she dutifully sprinkled the magical herbs over the water. In her heart, she knew she had done what her father and grandfather would have wanted, but despairingly she looked to her right to see her father no longer grasped in the golden dragon's claws. All of a sudden, there was a gigantic implosion of water. The water exploded as the samurai and oni simultaneously disappeared, as well as Boar-acc. In his place, next to Windwalker, stood a beautiful female dragon that batted her eyes amorously at Windwalker.

Sensei sat down on the ground at the edge of the fountain side in the puddles of water that remained. The giant Buddha face, which had been thrown high into the sky during the explosion, stood upright, embedded in the earth at the edge of the fountain. Looking about, they could see the tanuki and crows returning with chrysanthemum petals that they lay in front of Sensei and Natsumi in a path. They bowed and waited for Natsumi to dismount. As Natsumi did, the golden dragon suddenly approached and stood next to Sensei, rubbing her chin affectionately on him.

"Sensei, what are you doing?" Natsumi demanded.

"The golden dragon is really my old mate from centuries ago that was under a spell," Sensei answered. "And your father was really just an apparition to trick you. It was just an illusion. He's probably down by the television station as we speak. But if you had not made the decision that you did, none of us would be here."

"Yes, I am proud of you, Natsumi, and Toshi, too," a familiar voice said behind her.

Natsumi turned to see her grandfather's vision smiling back at her and alongside him was Snowflake. She and Toshi watched as their glowing images began to fade.

"We will always be with you," they could hear Snowflake's voice say, as they faded away into the night.

Natsumi and Toshi looked about at the mess strewn about.

"Now what?" Natsumi asked.

"Now, we dragons will take drinks of the magically charged water and sprinkle it about the world, and peace will remain forever, as long as there are dragons," Sensei answered.

"And there ought to be plenty more dragons now that there are two females," Windwalker chimed in. "Why don't you gather Bilbo and Cody and we'll give you all a ride home."

And so it was that Sensei and Windwalker dropped Natsumi, Toshi, Bilbo, and Cody off, safely at their attic window.

As Sensei accepted a hug from Natsumi, he fondly bade goodbye. "We will visit you each year at festival time. Until then, we wish you good luck, and if ever you need us, just call Snowflake or Grandfather Riujin and they will find us."

In so saying, the four watched as their two dragon friends flew off and joined the other two dragons that waited for them.

"I will miss them," Cody sighed.

"But won't life be nice without all that excitement?" Bilbo asked.

"And don't forget," Juliet offered from within the cage, "they promised they would visit us at festival time."

Natsumi and Toshi put the two rabbits back into their respective cages and closed the door as they tiptoed downstairs.

Passing by their parents' bedroom, they peeked inside to see the shapes of both their mother and their father, fast asleep.

Then they both turned toward their respective rooms, but not before Toshi admitted, "It will be nice not to have to watch our backs all the time. "Natsumi, how did you know to let Sensei crush the pearl?"

"Grandfather had told me a riddle that I didn't understand. He said, 'When all the world depends on you, you must give up what is all important to save what is most important.' I never understood until that moment what it meant. And when I read my fortune in Asakusa it said, World Peace depends on you. The true pearl is within you, and on this, the world depends. All at once, I understood why I had been told those things," Natsumi answered, as she turned into her room. "Goodnight, Toshi."

"Goodnight, Natsumi."

They both went to bed for a long deserved rest. Inside the attic, the rabbits also lay down to sleep, with barely a thump to be heard.

Let the Games Begin
~~~~~~~~~~~~~~~~~~~~~~~~~~~~~
Chapter 12

It had been a month since they had last seen Sensei and Windwalker. Natsumi and Toshi were meeting Aiko and Jimmy at the game arcade for some fun. They brought Bilbo and Cody along in their backpacks as they had insisted on seeing the new pinball machines that had been fashioned after Natsumi's science show model.

Natsumi and Toshi had taken their favorite way to Ameyayokocho to the game arcade. But first, they stopped at Benton-do Temple to show their respects to the goddess of fortune. Bilbo and Cody watched as they first washed their hands and mouth at the fountain and then waved incense over their heads at the incense pot. Then they crept back into the book bags to hide as they watched them go up the steps to the temple. Bilbo loved the colorful red, gold, and green trim on the temple's entrance and even more so the green tiled curly architecture on the Chinese-styled roofs, but inside was even more amazing. There on the ceiling of the hallway entrance was a drawing of the golden dragon, exactly as he remembered it, with gray-blue accents.

Natsumi and Toshi took off their shoes and proceeded to clap their hands, bow, and ring the ring the bell in front of the red paper lantern in order to wake the goddess. As they then entered the inner chapel, they could see a bronze goddess statue enshrined in front of a gold set of doors. A taiko drum and many other mysterious objects surrounded all this. They watched as Natsumi and Toshi each made a wish and tossed coins into a chest-like structure and bowed. Upon leaving, Natsumi and Toshi purchased a tablet outside the inner chamber where they each wrote a wish and hung it outside. Bilbo thought of his friends Sensei and Windwalker and wished that they were doing well in their new lives.

Soon they were on their way down the lantern-lined pathway that led past the lily covered Shinobazu Pond and then down the quiet tree-lined sidewalk that led toward Ameyayokocho. It was like many a sunny day in Tokyo and a great day for a walk.

Crossing the street that separated Ueno Park from Ameyayoko Avenue, Bilbo and Cody could smell the sense of Ameyayokocho. Fish, shrimp, and pineapple…it had all become familiar to them. They could not help but love a culture that embraced the rabbit and the sense of peace. They could hear the street vendors calling out specials as they made their way.

Arriving outside the arcade entranceway, they could hear quite a commotion going on.

"There's Aiko and Jimmy!" Natsumi cried out.

"Hi, Toshi! Hi, Natsumi! We've all been waiting for you!" Aiko blurted out, as she pointed to a young enthusiastic man. "This is the DJ for Radio Japan; he's here to announce your new game, Pinball for World Peace.

"Everyone, stand back," the man with a microphone in his hand said. "Here comes the games originator, Miss Natsumi Hashimoto, to dedicate the new pinball machine fashioned after her very own science project! Natsumi, would you do us the honor of playing the very first game?"

"I'd love to!" Natsumi exclaimed. As the DJ handed Natsumi a coin, she ceremoniously placed it into the coin slot and heard a loud clunk. Then she pulled the lever and a red colored ball sprung out. The game immediately played the melody that Bilbo, Cody, and she had written for the game.

"Hey, little bunny, watcha gonna do, when all those critters are after you. First the hawk and then the hog, now Japan seems just as bad. Better run boy, run and hide boy, it seems that trouble is on your tail. Get your friends now, your newfound friends and how, that's all you'll need to save the day!

They watched as the pinball bounced around the scenes of the dragon and tanuki chasing the rabbit through the Shinobazu Pond and chasing after the rabbit and his jewels. Then the ball hit the center area that depicted the grand fountain explosion, which then popped open and displayed the dragon and tanuki holding paws with the Bilbo Bunny. Then out of the game's portal exit popped a gemlike souvenir token pinball with a bunny photo on it.

Natsumi picked up the pinball and held it up for all to see. When you looked very closely, you could see the words, Rabbits for World Peace.

"The first Bilbo Bunny game ball! Let the games begin!" the DJ called out over the loudspeaker. Throughout the arcade room, they could hear the coin droppings and the ding-dings of the pinball's hitting the bells and music. Before long, Natsumi, Toshi, Aiko, and Jimmy had played for an hour and left the arcade for the Hashimoto's to stay overnight.

"Natsumi, could you tell us more stories tonight?" Aiko asked.

"Yes, we'll all go up to the attic, play with the rabbits, tell stories, and wait to see if there are any dragons in the sky under the skylight," Natsumi replied.

"And don't forget! We'll play the new electronic pinball game on the TV," Toshi said.

"Sounds like fun, don't you think?" Bilbo squealed from out of his backpack to Cody.

"Sure does. I can't wait to get back!" Cody replied.

As the six made their way through the Shinobazu Pond shortcut, the sun had already begun to set and they hurried to get home, but no longer were they fearful. Benton-do Shrine bore a welcome sight to them as it meant they weren't too far from home and the row of stone lanterns helped mark their way as they looked at the brilliant colors of the sunset that reflected upon the ducks that bobbed amongst the lily pads. The sound of the frogs made for a cheerful melody in the bewitchment of the oncoming twilight.

"Isn't Japan wonderful?" Bilbo said to Cody.

"The best place I've been! I'm glad you're here with Natsumi and me."

"Me too," Bilbo agreed.

"How did that song go?" Toshi asked the others.

"Like this," replied Natsumi as she lead them in song…

"Hey, little bunny, watcha gonna do, when all those critters are after you. First the hawk and then the hog, now Japan seems just as bad. Better run boy, run and hide boy, it seems that trouble is on your tail. Get your friends now, your newfound friends and how, that's all you'll need to save the day!

Circle of Friends

Friends Forever